Deadloc

Anna Conway, rising twenty, had much to live for: a pleasant home, a devoted young husband who put her welfare before all else. Yet she suffered from depression and, just before leaving on a restorative cruise, she was found dead.

Chief Inspector Kelsey and Sergeant Lambert at first accepted Anna's death as suicide, and the more they learned of her childhood, the more understandable suicide became. So it was with shock that they learned that when Anna married David she was already the widow of an elderly man, whose death was not without unusual features.

But when they learned that David Conway too had been a widower, his first wife having also committed suicide, Kelsey developed a gut feeling that this grief-stricken widower was a murderer. Yet there was ample testimony to his devotion to Anna, his alibi was unimpeachable and his motive for her murder non-existent.

Doggedly the Chief Inspector set out to prove David's guilt. But each time he unearthed a suspicious circumstance, David came up with an innocent explanation.

Move, counter-move. Deadlock. Had Kelsey met his match at last? The denouement is swift and shattering. This is Emma Page at her best.

EMMA PAGE

Deadlock

THE CRIME CLUB
An Imprint of HarperCollins *Publishers*

First published in Great Britain in 1991
by The Crime Club, an imprint of
HarperCollins Publishers, 77–85 Fulham Palace Road,
Hammersmith, London W6 8JB

04860758

British Library Cataloguing in Publication Data

Page, Emma
Deadlock
I. Title
823.914[F]

ISBN 0 00 232345 1

Photoset in Linotron Baskerville by
Rowland Phototypesetting Ltd
Bury St Edmunds, Suffolk
Printed and bound in Great Britain by
HarperCollins Book Manufacturing, Glasgow

For J.B. and B.B.
in gratitude

CHAPTER 1

The brass plate beside the front door of Dr Peake's hand-some Edwardian premises, half a mile beyond the north-western tip of Cannonbridge, glittered in the mellow sunshine of late afternoon.

Sunlight flashed from the doctor's gold-rimmed spectacles as he strolled along the peaceful walks of his beloved garden in the welcome lull before evening surgery—on Tuesdays surgery began at six.

He glanced about with pleasure. Still plenty of colour in the flowerbeds and borders for the first week in September. He paused to savour the delicate fragrance of a rose. A silver-haired man with a spare, upright figure, a look of buoyant optimism undimmed after long years in general practice.

He looked at his watch. Time he was getting back indoors. He let himself in through the conservatory, into the cool interior, along the corridor into the entrance hall.

At the window in reception he saw the husband of a patient—Conway, yes, that was the name. Mrs Conway had consulted him for the first time a couple of months ago; she and her husband had come to live in a neighbouring hamlet back in the spring.

Conway was picking up a repeat prescription for his wife. 'Hello, there!' the doctor called out as he came up behind him. 'How's your wife? More relaxed and cheerful, I hope?'

David Conway turned from the window. He had a direct, open glance. On the tall side, with a slim, athletic build. Still boyish-looking, although a year or so past thirty. A square jaw, a broad forehead with a lock of fair hair falling forward. Well-groomed, smartly dressed in a business suit, shoes polished to a mirror finish.

He smiled at the doctor. 'Anna's much improved, I'm

glad to say. And she's sleeping a lot better.' He put the prescription away in his pocket.

'That's good,' Peake said heartily. Patients were beginning to drift in. He nodded to one or two, spoke a word here and there. He moved away from reception with Conway and stood talking to him further down the hall. 'I'll look in on your wife next time I'm over your way—but don't for heaven's sake tell her that or she'll work herself up into a stew every morning, wondering if it'll be today I'll be calling in.' He paused. 'Is she getting out much?'

Conway shook his head. 'Not very much, I'm afraid.'

'That's got to be altered,' Peake pronounced briskly. 'She's at a time of life when she should be full of plans for the future. She should be enjoying making new friends, a whole new life. If you could get her to start thinking positively along those lines it would do her more good than any amount of sleeping pills and anti-depressants.' A thought struck him. 'Does she drive?'

Conway shook his head again. 'She's never shown any inclination to learn.'

'Then start teaching her. She'll fall in with anything you suggest. Could be the very thing for her. Living out in the country, on her own all day, it's easy for any woman to get shut in on herself, stuck at home without transport. It'll give her a new interest, something to aim at.'

He clapped Conway on the shoulder. 'And if you could manage a little second-hand car for her, that would encourage her even more. You needn't pay the earth for it. Once she's passed her test she'll be able to drive into town every day, even if it's only to do a bit of shopping, change her books at the library. It's all human contact, it all helps.'

'You're absolutely right!' Conway responded with energy. 'I should have thought of it myself, it's a first-class idea. I'll get cracking on it right away.'

'And talking about getting out more—' Peake suddenly broke off. He excused himself and went swiftly along to assist an elderly patient hobbling in with the aid of a stick. He returned to take up again where he'd left off, all the while keeping a benevolent eye open all round. 'As I was saying, would it be possible to arrange a holiday for your wife? That often does the trick, better than any amount of tranquillizers.'

'Do you think she's up to it yet?' Conway asked in a tone of anxiety. 'It would mean she'd have to go on her own. There's no chance of my being able to get away at this time of year.' He had been in his present job, with Zodiac Soft Furnishings, only since March. He had no leave due to him as yet, and one of the firm's two busiest seasons was already under way.

'I wasn't suggesting she went right away,' Peake demurred. 'In a few weeks' time was what I had in mind. I'm sure she'll be up to it by then. And I wasn't suggesting she went on her own. Isn't there some relative or friend who could go with her?'

Conway pondered. 'I can't think of anyone who could get away.'

'Then a cruise is your answer,' Peake returned with undiminished gusto. 'Just the thing late in the year. You can head for the sun, shorten the winter.'

'A cruise?' Conway echoed doubtfully.

'Don't look so surprised.' Peake smiled. 'People have very out-of-date notions about cruises if they haven't been on one recently. They've changed out of all recognition over the last ten or fifteen years. It's not all old fogies these days, plenty of young folk go on cruises now, families too. My wife and I have been on a good many cruises over the years and we've enjoyed every one of them. There's never any need to feel lonely, they're ideal for folk on their own, convalescing. No pressure, no need to do anything you don't feel like. You can lie about all day if you want to. Nothing to worry about, everything done for you. Doctor and nurses if you happen to need them. Your wife will love it. Sea, sunshine, change and stimulation, wonderful food. Meeting new people, striking up friendships, finding new interests.'

He suddenly ground to a halt, conscious he'd got rather carried away. A young couple like the Conways, living in a rented, furnished bungalow, hoping to be able to buy a place of their own, were hardly likely to have much to spare for fancy extras like cruises.

'Of course cruises don't come cheap.' Peake's tone held apology. 'And she would really need to go for two or three weeks to do much good.' He looked inquiringly at Conway. 'I suppose that would be out of the question?'

'If a cruise is what you recommend,' Conway responded with decision, 'then that's what Anna's going to have. I'll manage the money, whatever it costs. All I want is to see her well and happy, that's more important than any other consideration.'

Peake delivered another hearty slap on the back. 'Good man. You won't regret it.'

Conway gave a wry grin. 'Just as well I can't go with her. I should be able to manage one ticket but two would be a bit of a facer.'

'I'm willing to bet we'll see a substantial improvement when she gets back,' Peake told him bracingly.

'And if we don't?'

Peake grimaced. 'Then we might have to think about seeing a psychiatrist.' He raised a hand as Conway opened his mouth. 'Yes, yes, I know. I'm well aware she's dead set against seeing a psychiatrist but I'm sure between us we could manage to talk her into it.'

Conway smiled slightly. 'I was going to say I entirely agree with you. I think Anna should see a psychiatrist if the cruise doesn't do the trick.'

'Good man,' Peake said again. He glanced at the clock. 'Off you go now—and don't forget to see about that cruise. Don't ask your wife's opinion about it, present her with a *fait accompli*. Make the booking and then tell her you've got a wonderful surprise for her. Produce the tickets, get out an atlas, show her all the places on the map, get her enthusiastic about it. That's always the best way with nerve cases. Never give them a choice, the chance to say no. Firm direction's a great relief to folk in that state of mind. Trying to make any kind of decision can be agony for someone who's anxious enough already.'

As he turned towards his surgery he couldn't refrain from adding, 'And tell her you'll buy her some new clothes for the trip, that's always a sure-fire tonic for the ladies. Throw in a new hair-do while you're at it. She'll agree to go all right, you'll see. And when she gets back she'll have Christmas to look forward to, the start of a new year, spring on the way.'

Ferndale, the bungalow rented by the Conways, was a substantial dwelling, built between the wars. It stood in an isolated spot in the scattered hamlet of Oldmoor, a few miles to the north-west of Cannonbridge.

The weather in the second week of September was no less fine than in the first. At two o'clock on Tuesday afternoon Anna Conway came to the end of the household chores she had managed to spin out since breakfast. She stood at the back door of the bungalow, staring out into the brilliant, windless afternoon, trying to make up her mind how to pass the next hour or two.

If she had been less willow-wand thin, with less of a look of being huddled into herself against the cold, however warm the day, she might have been pretty enough. Her small features were regular, her baby-fine hair a pleasant shade of light brown, her grey eyes large and well set. As it was, she would never catch the attention of a casual ob-server, unless perhaps to wonder fleetingly how a girl of her age—rising twenty—had acquired so early so apprehensive a stance towards life.

She twisted her hands together. The garden seemed so still, waiting, watching. What she longed to do was take a sleeping pill, crawl into the big double bed and pull the covers over her head, extinguishing for the next few hours every nerve, every thought and feeling, every lacerating memory.

But yesterday evening, as they sat close together on the sofa, David had slipped an arm round her shoulders, had gently suggested she might like to occupy some of the time that hung so heavily on her hands with a little leisurely tidying up of the flowerbeds and borders. The exercise could only do her good and he would be glad of any help, however small, in putting to rights the large, rambling garden, neglected by a succession of tenants.

The thought of being able to greet him on his return this evening with the news that she had indeed spent the afternoon battling with weeds, being able to point out some patch of ground she had cleared, seeing his smile of pleasure, hearing his praise, finally won out over the lure of temporary oblivion.

And Dr Peake would be pleased too, next time he saw her. Fresh air and sunshine, he always urged, useful activity of any kind.

She squared her shoulders and stepped out into the caressing air, closing the door resolutely behind her. She went with determined steps over to a shed, wheeled out a barrow, selected a hoe, hand fork, trowel, a pair of shears, pulled on stout gardening gloves.

She looked about for an area to tackle, not too intimidating, and settled on part of a long flower border overrun with golden rod and marguerites. She began to tear up handfuls of rank growth.

The garden no longer seemed so silent. Sounds now seemed to press in on her from every side, obscurely tinged with menace. The raucous cawing of rooks, an aeroplane droning high overhead, the distant yapping of a dog, the harsh whine of a chainsaw, intermittent bursts of shooting from a neighbouring farm.

She worked grimly on till her back began to ache, then she abandoned the border and set off on a tour of the garden.

In the long grass of the orchard area drunken wasps

buzzed among rotting windfalls. Every tree appeared ancient and diseased, bearing misshapen apples, grotesque pears. On the edge of the shrubbery, beneath a vast old hydrangea still in bloom, she caught sight of a great clump of oyster-coloured fungus, like a mound of overlapping dinner plates. She stopped in fascinated horror to peer under bushes and shrubs. Even larger clumps of fungus greeted her, rubbery and warty.

She shuddered and plunged on. Long strands of bramble clutched at her clothes. At the base of a decaying tree-stump she came on an enormous fleshy growth dissolving into slime, its stalk alive with maggots. Panic stirred inside her but she thrust it sternly down. She darted out into a stretch of open ground, came to a halt. She drew deep breaths, striving to steady herself.

She would go back to her flower border, show some backbone, start again on her task. She walked determinedly over to where she had abandoned her tools, picked up the hand fork and began to lever up stubborn roots.

But revulsion welled up again inside her. Centipedes squirmed in the earth, daddy-long-legs brushed against her face. A horrid sensation, only too familiar of late, signalled its return with a first stealthy touch as of a band lightly circling her forehead. She tried to dismiss it, went on battling with the weeds.

Slowly the band began to tighten. Across the fields a fresh burst of shooting jerked her up in fright. She managed to steady herself again, bent once more to her task.

A few moments later a wounded pigeon dropped out of the sky at her feet in a sprawl of blood-stained feathers. She sprang back in terror. Tears spilled from her eyes. She threw down her fork, tore off her gloves. She fell to her knees beside the dying bird, gently stroked its head, crooned softly to it. It looked up at her with an expressionless eye already filming over. A moment later she saw that it was dead.

She jumped up, snatched her gloves, the tools, and raced back to the shed, her heart pounding, leaping in her throat.

With trembling fingers she restored everything to its place, then she turned and fled back to the house, along glinting gravel paths where leaf shadows quivered in the sunlight, past bushes festooned with spiders' webs, in through the back door, along the passage, into the haven of the sitting-room.

She flung herself down on the sofa, shuddering. From the mantelpiece her own likeness—a framed photograph, head and shoulders—looked down at her with a wide smile of happiness.

Around her forehead the band grew vice-like in its grip. A surge of terrifying thoughts rose in her brain, threatening to overwhelm her. She looked in agony at the clock. Another hour to be lived through before the next dose of the pills that would beat back the thoughts. David had made her swear to stick to the prescribed times and amounts. Every day she strove to keep her word, she never let him know of the many times she failed.

She turned her head in the direction of the kitchen. A beaker of the hot chocolate she loved, strong and sweet, that might soothe her through the next hour. She got up and went from the room.

Twenty minutes later found her back in the sitting-room, pacing to and fro, the effects of the hot chocolate already evaporated. She tried to distract herself with the radio, the television, but they served only to jangle her nerves still further.

She looked again at the clock. She would not fail again. She lay down on the floor and closed her eyes. She went religiously through her tense-and-relax exercises, she massaged her forehead, her scalp, the back of her neck. Still the taut muscles refused to slacken. Still the plaguing thoughts bedevilled her brain.

She opened her eyes and looked yet again at the clock. Barely ten minutes had crawled by. She could struggle no longer. She got to her feet and went along to the bedroom for the capsules, the pills and tablets. She washed down the prescribed dose with water, then she stood hesitating, eyeing the bottles. Double the quantity would produce the longed-for relief twice as quickly.

After another brief, guilt-ridden struggle she swallowed a second dose. She went back to the sofa and lay down again. Soon she felt a blissful peace begin to steal over her. A little later she felt a slight resurgence of cheerfulness; later still, a burst of buoyant energy.

She sat up, smiling. She yawned, stretched luxuriously. She went along to the bathroom, washed her face, tidied her hair. She would make a start on preparing supper.

As the hands of the kitchen clock approached six she was putting the finishing touches to an artistically arranged platter of salad. A delicious savoury smell filled the room. She glanced in at the oven, lifted the lids of pans simmering on the stove. She felt joyously serene. Her mind was now clear and untroubled. She hummed in tune with the music from the radio.

A sound reached her ears: David's car turning in through the gate. Her face broke into a delighted smile. She darted to the mirror, primped her hair.

She ran out of the kitchen, along the passage, into the hall, snatched open the door into the porch. As David came hurrying round from the garage she flew out to greet him, threw her arms round his neck. He embraced her warmly, gave her a tender kiss.

Later, as they finished clearing the supper things, he put his arm round her shoulders. 'I've something to tell you,' he said in indulgent tones. 'Something to show you. I've arranged a wonderful surprise for you.' Her face lit up like a child at Christmas. He squeezed her shoulders. 'I know you're going to love it. Come and sit down, I'll tell you all about it.'

CHAPTER 2

A dark Monday morning, October 23rd. The birds not yet awake, only the occasional mournful cry of an owl.

On their smallholding, two miles from Ferndale, Bob and Irene Garbutt had been up since five; always plenty of indoor jobs to be done before sunrise.

At six-thirty Garbutt came out of the warm kitchen into the chill air, bending his head against the whipping breeze. A tall, broad-shouldered man, lean and solidly muscled. He had been a regular soldier, both his sons were in the Army.

As he crossed the yard a cock crowed shrilly in the distance. A lively cackling erupted from the wire-fronted sheds housing the geese. Garbutt glanced at his watch—he was due at Ferndale at five past seven to pick up David Conway and drive him to Oldmoor station, a regular booking since April, one Monday in four. Garbutt supplemented what he made from the smallholding by running a one-man hired-car service locally.

He went into the cold store for the box of fruit Conway had ordered for his wife. Garbutt had selected the fruit with particular care the previous evening: sweetly-smelling Cox's orange pippins, prime Comice pears.

He carried the box out to his car and stowed it away in the boot. He went back into the house and stood washing his hands at the sink. Irene came into the kitchen, carrying a jar of her newly made damson jam. Still a pretty woman, with bright blue eyes and a ready smile.

She set the jam down on the table. 'You can take this for Anna, a little present to say I hope she's feeling better.'

Garbutt ate a piece of toast and drank a mug of tea; time for a decent breakfast later. Promptly at ten minutes to seven he got into his car. He prided himself on punctuality and reliability. No need to allow for delays; scarcely any traffic on these rural roads at this time of day, this season of the year.

The sky showed the first signs of lightening as he turned the car towards Ferndale; birds began to twitter from the hedgerows.

The front of the bungalow was in darkness when he pulled up by the recessed porch but a light shone out from the kitchen, round to the left. He tooted his horn and Conway appeared a minute or two later, switching lights on as he came. He found Garbutt standing by the open boot of his car, lifting out the box of fruit.

'Anna'll be delighted with those,' Conway exclaimed as he cast an appreciative eye over the unblemished skins. 'What do I owe you?'

'No need to bother with that now.' Garbutt set the box down inside the porch. 'Leave it till this evening. We can settle up then.' Conway was travelling to Dunstall—home of Zodiac's factory and head office—for the four-weekly sales meeting. Garbutt usually picked him up again at Oldmoor station at a quarter to one but today was the firm's silver jubilee, to be marked, following the sales meeting, by festivities lasting well into the afternoon.

Garbutt handed over the jam, along with his wife's message. 'That's very good of Irene,' Conway said with pleasure. He carried the fruit and jam inside and Garbutt got back into his car, out of the wind.

A few minutes later Anna came out into the shelter of the porch. She wore a blue woollen dressing-gown and bedroom slippers.

'The fruit's lovely,' she told Garbutt with a warm smile. The porch light threw shadows over her face and hair. She reached into a pocket for a handkerchief and dabbed at her lips. 'And please thank Irene for the jam, it's very kind of her. Damson's one of my favourites. Tell her I'm feeling much better.'

'I'm delighted to hear it,' Garbutt responded heartily. 'You can start eating the Coxes any time but I should give

the pears another day or two. You'll want to keep your eye
on them, catch each one just right, when it's sweet and
juicy.'

'I'll remember.' She thrust her hands into her sleeves for
warmth, like a Chinese mandarin.

'Not long now till your holiday,' Garbutt commented.

'November 2nd, a week on Thursday.' Her tone was
pleased and lively. 'I'm really looking forward to it now.'

Conway came back, wearing a short tweed overcoat. He
carried a briefcase and a pair of gloves. He caught the tail
end of their conversation.

'I'm driving Anna down to Southampton,' he told Garbutt. 'I'm meeting her there again when the ship docks.'
Anna looked up at him with a loving smile. 'We're going
shopping on Wednesday,' Conway added. 'To buy her some
gorgeous clothes for the trip. I've fixed it so I've got the
whole afternoon free. We're going into Cannonbridge.' He
named a large department store. 'We're taking it easy, doing
it all under one roof, breaking off for tea in the café half way
through, so she won't be worn out at the end of it. I intend
it to be a pleasure, not an ordeal.'

Anna turned her head and smiled at Garbutt. 'I'm really
being spoiled, don't you think? I shall enjoy choosing the
clothes, though I'm not going to be too extravagant.'

Conway put his arm round her shoulders and kissed her
tenderly. 'Don't stand out here in the cold. I'll be home
around a quarter to seven. And don't go wearing yourself
out, doing too much housework. You've got the place looking spotless already.'

'No, I won't.' Her mouth opened suddenly in a deep
yawn and she put up a hand to cover it. 'I'll make sure I
get plenty of rest. There's a film on TV this afternoon I'm
going to watch, it should be good. And I might go out for
a stroll if the wind drops.' Conway smiled approval.

But she didn't go back inside at once. She kept her gaze
fixed on her husband as he got into the passenger seat.

Garbutt switched on the ignition. His watch showed

seven-fifteen. Anna stood smiling and waving as the car reversed and drove out into the lane.

The instant it vanished from sight the smile left her face, her hand dropped to her side. She shivered, pulled her dressing-gown closely round her. She sent a long, lingering look round the shadowy garden, the dark trees, the paling sky. Then she reached out and switched off the outside light. She turned and went slowly back into the house, closing the door behind her.

Oldmoor station lay one and a half miles from Ferndale on a stretch of line closed thirty years ago, later rescued from vandalism and dereliction by a preservation society which raised funds, laboured to restore it, acquired and refurbished old rolling-stock, repaired the buildings.

Now, fifteen years after the first rejuvenated steam train rode the rails, the society operated—with the aid of extra income from occasional filming and TV commercials—a successful and established schedule, highly popular with local travellers as well as holidaymakers and steam enthusiasts. The line linked up with the main railway system at Sedgefield Junction where a fast train would carry Conway on to Dunstall.

'A shame to get Anna out of bed so early,' Garbutt remarked as he negotiated a bend in the road.

'She would get up to speak to you,' Conway said. 'I told her there was no need, I could pass on her message, but no, she must thank you and Irene herself.'

'It's good to see her so much brighter. And ready for her holiday.' Garbutt slid a glance at Conway. 'The holiday must be costing you a bob or two, new clothes and all.'

'If it helps to get her really well again, it's worth every penny.' Conway grimaced. 'When I think how she was, back in the summer—some days she didn't get up out of bed at all. She wouldn't even bring the milk in from the back door or the newspaper from the front porch.' His tone echoed the anxiety of that distressing time. 'I'd know as soon as I drove up in the evening if it had been one of her worst days. The paper would still be on the bench in the porch.' He shuddered briefly. 'But we're well past that now, thank God. Dr Peake's been very good to her. And she's tried very hard herself, I must give her that.'

'Occupation,' Garbutt declared with robust conviction. 'That's the answer. Look at Irene. Lots of women her age, children grown up and left home, they get to feeling sorry for themselves. They sit around moping, swallowing pills or taking to booze, I don't know which is worse. Irene hasn't got time to invent worries for herself. She's busy from morning till night, she loves every minute of it.'

Conway suddenly raised a hand. 'I meant to ask you— it's Anna's birthday next Monday, the 30th. I'd like a good house plant, or maybe Irene could make me up a bouquet— I don't know what she's got in the way of flowers this time of year. I could pick up the plant or the bouquet on Sunday evening, put it somewhere cool overnight where Anna won't see it.'

'I'm sure Irene'll be able to find you something to suit you,' Garbutt told him. 'She's got some first-class house plants coming on. Or she could make up an indoor garden. They're a bit more unusual and they last a long time. The best thing would be if you had a word with Irene yourself. Drop in one evening on your way home, see what's on offer.'

'Right, thanks,' Conway said. 'I'll do that.'

They reached the station in good time. The buildings were beautifully decorated; elegant old bracket lamps shed a golden glow. A striking display of purple and white dahlias graced island beds set in the twin platforms.

Passengers strolled up and down, chatting in friendly fashion, looking about with keen attention as they waited for the train. No stand-offishness here, no grimly silent Monday-morning faces. Everywhere an air of holiday gaiety, even among those clearly on their way to an ordinary day's work.

Garbutt got out of the car and went into the station with

Conway, as he always did. His boyhood love of steam trains was as strong as ever.

'I wish I could spare the time to put in half a day here now and then,' he said when Conway came back from buying his ticket.

'I wouldn't mind putting in more time myself,' Conway told him. He came along most weekends, with an occasional extra stint in the lighter evenings.

The signal dropped. The passengers stopped perambulating and lined the platform, craning to catch the first plume of smoke, ears cocked for the distant rumble of wheels.

She came swooping down on them with a heart-stirring rush and roar, the engine splendid in green and black livery, brasswork gleaming, coaches brilliant in scarlet and cream. Along the open windows, men and women leaned out, smiling and waving. Among them, a lad of seventeen or so, scrutinizing the waiting passengers as the train swept in. He caught sight of Conway, his face broke into a cheerful grin. He called out a greeting, lost in the medley of sounds.

Conway raised a hand in reply and hastened along the platform to where the lad's compartment would stop. The train drew to a halt amid clangs and hisses. Doors swung open. Garbutt stood watching the lively to-and-fro with his eyes alight, savouring the acrid scents of steam and smoke.

'Pick you up at six-thirty,' he called out as Conway stepped aboard. Conway turned and waved, gave him a nod. The lad closed the door. The guard waved his flag, blew his whistle.

On the dot of seven thirty-two the engine began to snort and grunt. Along with everyone else remaining on the platform, Garbutt stood motionless as the train pulled out, slow and stately. He stayed gazing after it till its lights had vanished into the shadowy distance and the far-off rattle of its wheels was lost among the rising sounds of morning.

CHAPTER 3

The sky was still flushed from sunset when Garbutt halted his car again at Oldmoor station. His watch showed six-ten. Time for a pleasurable stroll round, a good look at every detail, every notice.

He pulled his coat collar about his ears as he got out of the car. Bitterly cold in the wind. At least the rain was holding off.

Promptly at six-thirty the brightly lit train came thundering in. Conway leaned out of a window, gave Garbutt a cheery wave. The train clattered to a stop in the lamplit dusk. Conway jumped down and joined Garbutt under the shelter of a canopy. They stood watching the animated bustle till the train huffed and puffed its way out again, spot on time.

Whirls of coppery leaves danced along the road in the car's headlamps as they drove out to Ferndale. Lights shone out from scattered dwellings. Conway chatted about his day at the factory. The festivities had been a trifle long-winded for his taste, the speeches a shade self-congratulatory. But it had been enjoyable enough. The sales meeting in the morning had gone particularly well. Plenty of good offers, first-class job lots of materials bought in against the demands of the advancing season.

'You remember Irene asking me a few weeks ago about new curtains and bedspreads for the back bedroom?' Conway said.

Garbutt nodded. 'That's right. She'd like them for the New Year. The eldest son and his family should be due some leave. They'll be home from Germany around then.'

'I promised Irene I'd let her know when we had some good discount offers. I should be able to fix her up now. We've got some exceptionally good promotion lines specially

for the jubilee. I'll be very surprised if she can't find something she likes among them. If you've got ten minutes to
spare you can pop into the house with me now, take a look
at the swatches.

'If you think any of them might suit, you can take them
home with you, Irene can look through them this evening.
I'll pick them up first thing in the morning. If she does
decide to place an order I'll take it then, I can get the order
pushed through right away. You've got to be quick off the
mark with these specials, they get snapped up pretty fast,
they're terrific value.'

'Sounds just the job.' Garbutt was pleased. 'I'll come in
and take a look at the patterns now. I've nothing on till
seven-thirty, that's when I pick up my old gent to take him
along to his club. Irene's been very satisfied with the covers
you got her for the sitting-room, back in the summer.'

'That's settled, then,' Conway said. 'And I can have a
word with Irene in the morning about the flowers for Anna's
birthday.'

There were no lights visible as they approached Ferndale.
Garbutt pulled up by the front door and they got out of the
car. Conway switched on the porch light. Garbutt wiped
his feet on the mat.

Conway stood rigid for a moment, frowning at the sight
of the morning paper still lying folded on the side bench,
but he made no comment. He picked up the paper, bent it
in two and thrust it into the slant pocket of his overcoat. He
set down his briefcase and pulled off his gloves, got out his
keys.

'Anna's probably having a nap,' he said as he unlocked
the front door. His tone strove for lightness. He raised a
cautionary hand to indicate the need for silence.

Cosy warmth floated out to welcome them as they stepped
into the hall. 'Come through into the kitchen,' Conway said
in a low voice. 'You can have a cup of tea while you look at
the patterns.'

Garbutt nodded and followed him along the passage to

the kitchen. Everything scrupulously clean and tidy. No sign of food preparation, no smell of cooking. A faint drift of music sounded from the direction of the bathroom.

Conway's face cleared. 'She's having a bath.' His voice held relief. 'I'll pop along and let her know we're here.' He waved a hand. 'Put the kettle on. Make yourself at home.' He went cheerfully off.

Garbutt picked up the electric kettle and filled it at the sink. He could hear Conway tapping on the bathroom door, calling out: 'I'm home, Anna.' A brief silence. Louder knocking, the doorknob rattling. Conway's voice raised, calling urgently: 'Are you all right, Anna?' Calling again, more loudly still. Rattling, knocking, calling.

Garbutt set down the kettle and went along to the bathroom. Conway threw him a distracted glance, his face creased in anxiety. Garbutt put his ear against the door panel. Total stillness at the other side, except for the tinkling tune from the radio.

'She's locked herself in,' Conway said in a voice brittle with tension. 'She never does that.' He suddenly jumped back and launched himself at the door, shoulder on. The solid structure stood unyielding.

'Let me,' Garbutt said. At his second powerful kick the door burst open.

The bathroom was in darkness except for the light filtering in from the passage and the rosy glow from an infra-red heater on the wall above the handbasin.

The two men remained for an instant in frozen silence, gazing in, then Conway raised a hand to pull the cord of the light switch. In the moment before his fingers touched the cord, Garbutt's eyes made out the pale form reclining in the bath.

The ceiling light sprang to life and Garbutt saw that the bath was full of blood.

CHAPTER 4

By eleven o'clock the wind was blowing half a gale. In an interview room in the main Cannonbridge police station a single overhead bulb cast a harsh white light over the bare furnishings. An uneasy combination of pine disinfectant and floral air freshener lent a quirky note to the cheerless surroundings.

The officer detailed to take David Conway's statement had now finished. He pushed back his chair. 'I'll see if they need you for anything more tonight,' he told Conway. 'If not, you'll be able to get off home.' He halted in the doorway. 'I'll try to find out what's happening about the post-mortem.'

Conway gave a nod. He slumped down in his seat, head lowered, eyes closed.

Some little time later, Police Constable Hamlin came along the corridor, at long last on his way home to bed. Greying hair, an air of shrewd common sense.

He paused by a window to assess the weather for the drive home. The sky was cloudless. A bright crescent moon lay on her back among glittering stars. The wind screamed round the building, tossing trees along the side of the forecourt.

There was no one else in the corridor and he permitted himself a gigantic yawn before moving off again. It had been a very long day. He had been driving back to Cannonbridge alone, shortly before seven, in the happy belief that he would soon be heading for home, when he got a message to go at once to Ferndale. A reported death, his was the nearest car. He had been first on the scene.

He blinked away the grim recollection. His long years in the force had hardened him to a great many things but not to everything. An appalling death for so young a woman.

A terrible thing, depression, so much more prevalent nowadays, it seemed, than when he was a young constable, starting out. So much more severe in so many cases, always to be taken very seriously indeed. And the poor husband, Conway, shattered and distraught, but still trying his best to he helpful and cooperative.

Hamlin turned a corner in the corridor. Ahead of him he saw with surprise the light still shining out through the glass-panelled door of the room where Conway had been interviewed. He'd have thought they'd have finished with Conway by now, let him get off home.

He reached the room, halted and looked in through the glass. Conway was alone, sitting at the table, leaning forward in an attitude of studious concentration, gazing intently down at a newspaper folded into a square.

He showed no sign of distress or agitation, he appeared oblivious of his bleak surroundings. He moved his mouth, bit his lip, as if deep in cogitation. From time to time he made a mark on the newspaper with a pen. He put Hamlin in mind of nothing so much as a man at a café table, marking runners on the racing pages.

Hamlin opened the door and stuck his head in. 'You still here, then?' he asked on a friendly note.

Conway laid down his newspaper and put the pen away in a breast pocket. He looked up at Hamlin, his face composed but infinitely weary. 'I've finished my statement,' he said flatly. 'I'm waiting to see if there's anything else.'

'I'll hang on, then,' Hamlin offered. 'I'm off home myself. I can give you a lift. You're not many minutes further along my own road.'

'That's very good of you.' Conway passed a hand over his eyes.

Footsteps sounded along the corridor. Hamlin turned his head and saw Detective Chief Inspector Kelsey approaching. He stepped smartly to one side of the open door.

The Chief gave him no more than a passing glance as he halted on the threshold. A big, solid man with a freckled face dominated by a large, fleshy nose. Carroty hair, thick and springing, the vibrant colour still untouched by grey. Bright green eyes; a penetrating look, even at this late hour.

'There's nothing more tonight,' the Chief informed Conway. 'You can get off home.' He gazed down at him with compassion. Pale and exhausted under the bright light, still with a boyish look.

'Will you be at home tomorrow?' Kelsey asked. 'Around lunch-time?'

Conway stared up at him with a lost air as if tomorrow was a stretch of time he couldn't begin to envisage. He gave a hesitant nod.

'We'll probably be in touch with you then,' Kelsey told him. 'We should have the results of the post-mortem.' Conway gave another slow nod.

'You'll want some transport,' Kelsey added.

Constable Hamlin stepped forward. 'I can give Mr Conway a lift home. I live out in that direction.'

'Right,' Kelsey said. Conway still sat motionless. He wore a poleaxed air as if rising from the table was beyond his powers.

'Don't sit up half the night brooding,' Kelsey advised. 'Going over things in your brain. Won't do any good. Try to get some sleep.' He bade them both good night and went back along the corridor.

Still Conway showed no sign of stirring. Hamlin went into the room and took Conway's coat from the back of a chair. He held it out.

'Come on,' he urged. 'Let's be off.'

Conway got slowly to his feet and put his arms into the coat. 'You'll want to button it up,' Hamlin said with a kindly air, as if to a child. 'It's bitter out.' Conway obediently buttoned up the coat, gazed about him, picked up the squared newspaper. He stuffed it into the pocket of his coat.

Hamlin ran an eye over him. He looked fit for nothing. 'Any friend or relative you could stay the night with?' he asked. 'I could give them a ring, explain matters. I don't mind running you wherever it is.'

Conway shook his head. 'Very good of you,' he said heavily, 'but I'll be all right, thanks. Got to face it some time.'

During the drive home Conway didn't speak. As they neared Ferndale he said, 'No need to drive in.'

Hamlin pulled up by the gate. 'Sure you'll be OK?' he asked as Conway opened the car door. 'Got something to help you sleep?'

'I'll be all right,' Conway said again. The wind tore at him. The crescent moon shed a pale radiance. Conway plunged through the stormy gusts to the front door.

Hamlin waited till the lights came on inside the bungalow, then he drove off. Poor devil, he thought with a shake of his head. I don't envy him the night he's got in front of him.

He went back along the way he had come, to his trim little semi in an outer suburb of Cannonbridge. The house was in darkness, his wife gone to bed. He drove into the garage with a minimum of noise. He got out, turned to close the car door.

Something white caught his eye—the folded newspaper, lying on the floor, half under the passenger seat. He reached over and picked it up.

He switched on the car's interior light and looked down at the paper. After a moment he raised his eyes and stared ahead, then he looked down again at the newspaper, frowning, pursing his lips.

CHAPTER 5

The wind had blown itself out in the night. At noon, brilliant yellow sunlight flooded in through the tall windows of the Cannonbridge General Hospital.

The pathologist came out of the mortuary, closing the

door on the echoing chill, the clinical smells, gleaming white tiles. Chief Inspector Kelsey waited for him along the corridor. They stood discussing the findings of the autopsy. Anna Conway had died from loss of blood. Both wrists had been neatly slit with a keen-edged instrument.

'A pocket knife,' Kelsey confirmed. They had found the open knife in the bath, its blades razor-sharp.

Conway had identified the knife as belonging to him. He had had it for some time, had scarcely ever used it. It was kept with other oddments in a small drawer of the dressing-table in the bedroom; the blades had always been very sharp. He clearly recalled drawing his wife's attention to the fact some weeks ago when he saw her picking up the knife. She had made no comment, had merely replaced the knife in the drawer.

The pathologist went on to say that Anna had ingested a quantity of assorted drugs, a mix of the standard medications she had been prescribed: anti-depressants, sleeping-pills, tranquillizers. A sizeable quantity but by no means a lethal dose, washed down with a milky chocolate drink, strong and sweet. There was nothing else in the stomach.

The effect of the drugs would be to induce a drowsy lethargy, drifting into a deep sleep, from which, in the ordinary way, she would have awakened in due course without ill effects.

Kelsey nodded as he listened. It all squared with what Conway had told them, that Anna had eaten and drunk nothing before he left the house at seven-fifteen yesterday morning. This was in accordance with Anna's usual practice. Conway regularly left for work while his wife was still in bed—as often as not, still asleep. It had never been his habit to take her a cup of tea or any other kind of hot drink in bed. She had never been accustomed to it, didn't want it.

Yesterday morning Anna had been woken by the arrival of Garbutt's car, the sound of voices. Conway told her about

the fruit, the present of jam. She had insisted on getting up
to thank Garbutt herself.

The pathologist was of the opinion that Anna had died
around an hour to an hour and a half after swallowing
the drugs and the chocolate drink. The delay had in all
probability been deliberate, to allow the medication time
to take effect, so that when she did step into the bath she
would feel no disabling agitation, would be able to deal
calmly enough with the unpleasant business of slitting her
wrists.

Kelsey cast his mind back to the estimated time of death
given to them by the police doctor summoned to Ferndale.
It was scarcely ever possible to be precise in such matters
but in the case of Anna Conway it was particularly difficult.
The bathroom was heated, the body had lain a considerable
time in water at first hot, gradually cooling. The doctor's
best estimate—and it could be no more than a very rough
estimate, he strongly emphasized—was that death had
occurred between eight and eleven on Monday morning.

The Chief was very much inclined to put the time of
death towards the latter rather than the earlier part of this
three-hour period. It had been a dark morning. There had
been no light on in the bathroom when Garbutt kicked the
door in. Anna would surely have switched the light on if
she'd gone into the bathroom before nine-thirty or ten.
Kelsey couldn't see a young woman like Anna Conway
taking her life in the dark.

It was well after one o'clock when Detective-Sergeant Lambert drove the Chief over to Ferndale to give Conway the
results of the autopsy. The Chief had eaten nothing since
a sketchy breakfast; post-mortems always destroyed his
appetite.

He gazed unseeingly out as they drove through the spec-
tacular colours of the autumn landscape. A fair proportion
of self-inflicted deaths would appear to be unintentional,
the attempt being in the nature of a cry for help, made in

the sure confidence of being found in time, dragged back from the brink. But some accident, some chance or whim takes a hand. The person cast all unknowing in the role of rescuer doesn't behave as expected. He meets a friend, stops for a chat. He is seized by hunger or thirst, he steps into a café. Or he merely catches a later bus than usual. The door opens too late, there is no rescue.

Then there was the other group, where the attempt was far removed from any kind of play-acting, very serious indeed, the would-be suicide making absolutely certain of not being found too early, not being dragged back, carefully choosing a time when there was no chance whatever of that door opening.

It seemed to Kelsey that Anna Conway's death fell unmistakably into that second category.

When they reached Ferndale Kelsey got out of the car and paused before pressing the doorbell. He glanced round the garden. It wore a melancholy appearance: ragged clumps of old perennials, untidy borders. A wheelbarrow half full of clippings was visible over by the shrubbery. On the ground beside it lay a billhook and a pair of shears.

Conway answered their ring at the door. He had been in the kitchen, clearing away the remains of a late lunch. He looked drained and apathetic but in control of himself.

He offered them coffee, asked if they had eaten—it wouldn't take him many minutes to knock up a few sandwiches. He couldn't offer them a drink, he didn't touch alcohol himself, never kept any in the house.

Kelsey declined the offer of sandwiches but would be glad of coffee. Conway carried the tray along to the sitting-room. He saw Kelsey's eye rest on the photograph of Anna on the mantelpiece.

'That was taken on our honeymoon.' Conway's voice strove for composure. 'We had a week by the sea in February.' He mentioned a sheltered resort on the South Coast. He looked across at the photograph. 'It was taken in one of those instant photo booths. That was the best one of her, I had it enlarged.' He handed round the coffee.

As Kelsey gave him the results of the autopsy Conway sat in silence, his head lowered. He looked up when the Chief had finished; distress showed clearly in his face.

'What time do you believe Anna took the pills?' His tone was urgent and unsteady. 'Do you think it was soon after I left the house?' A terrible thing to have to live with, Sergeant Lambert thought: someone so close to you on the very brink of self-destruction, but you noticed nothing out of the ordinary, you kissed her goodbye and went blithely off for the day, leaving her in that dreadful state of despair, utterly alone.

The Chief did his best to let Conway down gently. 'There's no reason to suppose it was soon after you left.' He explained in greater detail why it was impossible to be exact about timing. 'It could have been as late as nine-thirty when she took the tablets. She may have gone back to bed after you left. She could have dozed off, had a bad dream, perhaps, or woken in a fit of panic. She could have made her decision on a sudden impulse that you couldn't possibly have foreseen.'

The Chief shook his head. 'No way you can get inside someone else's head, fathom out their thought processes, however close you are to them. It does no good at all to start blaming yourself. There was no reason why you should have been able to guess what was in the wind.'

Conway's expression lightened fractionally.

'We'll let you know when the inquest's to be held,' Kelsey went on, adding that in all probability the body would at that time be released for burial.

He asked about Anna's parents and relatives. Did they live locally? Had they been informed of her death? Was there any way the police could help over that?

'I'm afraid I don't know about any relatives. None at all.' Conway's voice shook. 'I don't even know where Anna came from, where she lived as a child. She wasn't in touch with any of her family while I knew her. She would never talk about them. I don't even know if her parents are alive.'

He drew a trembling breath. 'As far as I could make out, she must have left home a few years back. I've no idea what the trouble was, she never spoke of it.'

He looked earnestly across at the Chief. 'I'm pretty sure the family situation, whatever it was, was at the bottom of her depression. I tried to get her to talk about it, I tried several times. I was sure it would help her, even if she found it painful. But she would never open up about it. She wanted to forget it completely. She was adamant about that.'

'We may need to get in touch with you again over the next day or two,' Kelsey said. 'There are always some points that need clearing up. When are you likely to be at home? What's the situation about your job?'

Conway told them he had spoken to Zodiac on the phone. They had been very understanding. He looked at Kelsey, his eyes full of pain. 'I didn't explain what had happened. All I told them was that my wife had died suddenly. I couldn't face going into details. They were very kind, they didn't ask any questions. I asked them not to say anything about it for the present to any of the workforce.' He drew another shuddering breath. 'The thought of being asked about it, people being sympathetic—' He shook his head. 'It would be more than I could stand right now.'

He had told Zodiac he wouldn't be working today and that he would probably have to take more time off in the immediate future. But he was anxious to get back to work as soon as possible.

'I've been trying to do a bit of gardening,' he told Kelsey, 'but it doesn't occupy my mind. And being here, on the premises, doesn't help. Being out at work would be a lot better.'

He closed his eyes briefly. 'Some kind of normal routine, being out and about all day, that would help me to stop

thinking, force me to concentrate on what I was doing.' And
he had a list of appointments, customers expecting him, he
never liked letting folk down.

If it was all right with the Chief Inspector he'd like to go
back to work in the morning. He would be at home every
evening after six, and every weekend, they could always
contact him then. If it was thought necessary on any
particular day he could always alter his schedule to call in
at the Cannonbridge police station.

'That all sounds very reasonable,' Kelsey agreed. 'I'm
sure you're right, work's by far the best thing for you just
now.' His tone took on a deprecating note. 'I'm afraid there
are one or two questions I must ask you now. Routine
questions, they've got to be asked in a case like this. I hope
you won't allow them to upset you too much.'

Conway gave a brief acknowledging nod.

'Had your wife made any similar attempt previously? Or
ever talked of making such an attempt?'

Conway shook his head with vigour. 'She never made any
kind of attempt to kill herself. She never threatened it, never
even hinted at such a thing. Never once. I never dreamed
for one single moment she'd ever contemplate—' He
dropped his head into his hands. Kelsey waited in com-
passionate silence till he had recovered himself.

'I'm sorry.' Conway took out a handkerchief and dabbed
at his face. 'I thought she was so much better,' he said
unsteadily. 'She seemed so much calmer and brighter. I was
so sure she'd be completely better before long. She was so
young, she had everything to look forward to.

'We planned to start a family after we'd found a place of
our own, that was something she wanted very much indeed.
We went looking at houses a lot when we first came here,
then we had to stop when she wasn't well, it was too much
of an effort for her. I hoped we'd be able to start looking
again quite soon.'

'Had your wife made a will?'

Conway nodded. 'We both made wills when we got

married. Very simple and straightforward, leaving everything to each other.'

'Was her life insured?'

He shook his head. 'No, it wasn't, she'd never taken out
any insurance on her life. I don't think it ever occurred to
her, it certainly never occurred to me. I took out a fairly
substantial term insurance on my own life when I got
married, so Anna would be all right if anything happened
to me. I'm on the road a good deal, there's always the risk
of an accident.' He shook his head again. 'But I never took
out any kind of insurance on Anna's life. I had no reason
to.'

Early afternoon somnolence brooded over the neighbourhood when Sergeant Lambert drew up before Dr Peake's
elegant villa. The doctor was expecting them after a phone
call from the Chief. He received them in his consulting
room; Anna Conway's file lay on the desk before him.

Anna had first called to see him towards the end of June;
she had come alone. It became clear in the course of the
visit that she hadn't told her husband she was consulting
him. She was clearly in a distressed state though she was
equally clearly exercising a considerable degree of self-
control. She complained of a fairly standard assortment of
nervous symptoms of varying degrees of severity.

At the end of the visit Dr Peake had asked her if she
didn't think it might be a good idea to bring her husband
into the picture, at least to the extent of telling him she was
seeking medical help. But she wouldn't hear of it.

'I spoke to her about it again the next time she came to
see me,' Peake added. 'That time she wasn't quite so decided
about it. She said she'd think it over.' On her third visit she
told him she'd spoken to her husband. He'd been very kind
and understanding. She seemed very relieved it was out in
the open.

Dr Peake had seen her four or five times since then and
he had also spoken to her husband more than once when

Conway had called in for repeat prescriptions for his wife.

Kelsey asked if he knew anything of Anna's family or background.

'I'm afraid I can't help you there.' Peake removed his gold-rimmed spectacles and polished them on a snowy handkerchief. 'She would never talk about her family— except to say that she no longer had anything to do with any of them. I tried to bring the matter up more than once but it upset her so much I thought it best to let it go—for the time being, at any rate.'

He gave Kelsey a direct look. 'She never confided in me about any personal matter. She hadn't come here in order to confide in me, she made that very plain. What she wanted was medication to deal with the symptoms that were troubling her.' He put his spectacles on again.

'I'm pretty sure from her reaction that it was the break with her family, and whatever had caused the break, that lay behind her anxiety and depression.' He leaned back in his chair. 'Of course the attempt to push the whole thing down below the level of conscious thought is counter-productive. It tends to blow the matter up out of all proportion. In the end it can start blotting out everything else.'

He looked reflective. 'I did suggest psychiatric help but she rejected that out of hand. I particularly thought hypnosis might be useful. I've seen excellent results where the patient has been trying to suppress the past, wouldn't open up, wouldn't respond to direct questioning.'

'It would be something from her childhood that Anna was suppressing?'

'Not necessarily. It might very well have been, but it could also have been something much more recent—or possibly a combination of the two. That's not uncommon, a disturbed childhood with later anxieties on top of it. In those cases the habit of suppression seems to be formed in childhood, it's resorted to again, later on, whenever anything traumatic takes place.' He waved a hand. 'As she wouldn't confide in me, all I can do now is make guesses.'

'How would you describe her personality?' Kelsey asked.

Peake put the tips of his fingers together. 'Average intelligence,' he said judicially. 'A naïve girl, immature for her age. Over-dependent, always ready to latch on to someone stronger, someone willing to take responsibility for her. A strong craving for security, for love and affection.'

He pursed his lips. 'It all ties in with this business of suppression, it's all part of the inability to face unpleasant facts, do something constructive about them, or at any rate, come to terms with them. The attempt to keep pushing them down out of the conscious mind prevents the personality developing, maturing. It interferes with normal healthy growth, emotional and psychological.'

He inclined his head. 'It doesn't help the learning process, either. With a youngster of school age you tend to get a pattern of unsatisfactory school reports, general lack of interest, poor concentration, inability to make friends. And there's often a history of being bullied.'

He had last seen Anna ten days ago when he had called in at Ferndale in passing, one morning. He had found Anna busy with household chores. She told him she felt a good deal better and was looking forward to her holiday. He was very pleased with her progress; she appeared much improved, calmer and more cheerful. No, he had never at any time considered her a suicide risk; there had never been the slightest hint of it. He had always been struck by her great determination to get well.

He sighed and shook his head. 'It's easy to be wise after the event. I believe now she was nowhere near as calm and cheerful as she made out, she was doing her best to put a good face on things. I believe she was terrified of going off alone on the cruise, even more terrified that she might have to face a psychiatrist if she came back from her holiday no better. I believe she was struggling very hard to master her fears, to force herself to do everything I had advised, everything her husband was encouraging her to do. She was determined not to let either of us down.'

He put a hand up to his face. 'It was entirely my idea, sending her off on a cruise. I persuaded poor Conway it would be money well spent.' He looked old and weary. 'It was all done with the best will in the world—and with this appalling result.'

He closed his eyes briefly. 'It doesn't bear thinking about, the crippling blow it must be for her husband. She thought the world of him and he was devoted to her. I don't think there's anything he wouldn't have done for her.'

He looked across at Kelsey. 'Men can get very critical of nervy wives, very short and snappy with them, downright abusive, sometimes. Some men walk out altogether. There was never anything like that with Conway, he was always kind and gentle. She was very appreciative, very anxious not to disappoint him. I think she wanted to get better for his sake as much as for her own.'

His look held great sadness. After the best part of a lifetime in medicine he was still deeply moved by the wastefulness of a young death. 'When one thinks of the total despair she must have felt—' He drew another sigh. 'Things can seem very black, very final, to the young.'

CHAPTER 6

The light was beginning to fade as Bob Garbutt drove on to the police station forecourt in good time for his four o'clock appointment; he had to make an official statement about his part in the dreadful discovery at Ferndale. At the bungalow yesterday evening there had been time for him to give only a brief verbal account to Constable Hamlin before he had to rush off to pick up his elderly gentleman, take him to his club.

He had spent a wretched night, had risen even earlier than usual, totally unrefreshed. All day he had smelled in his nostrils that stomach-turning blend of odours: rose-perfumed bath essence overlaid with the rank stench of blood.

He had been unable to blink away the grisly succession of sounds and images searing his brain. The terrible, piercing cry from Conway in the doorway of the bathroom, his horrified plunge forward at the bath. Anna's closed eyes in a face wax-white under the light; her pale, frail body in the crimson water.

Conway's frantic attempts to snatch at her slippery limbs, her puffed hands, haul her out of the bath in a futile effort to revive her, shouting at him to help. Himself dragging Conway back, holding him off. Anna so clearly dead, plainly dead for hours, long past any hope of resuscitation. To be left where she was, as she was—for other eyes to see.

Conway unable to take it in, plunging again at the bath, screaming at him to get an ambulance, a doctor, ring the hospital. Hauled forcibly back again, collapsing at last into a chair, crying and shaking, his head in his hands. Himself racing along to the phone in the front hall, to ring, not the ambulance, not the doctor or the hospital, but the police.

Garbutt got out of his car and made his way across the forecourt, up the steps and in through the doors. A short distance along the corridor leading out of reception, Constable Hamlin had made it his business to be hanging about, keeping an eye open for Garbutt. As soon as he saw him enter the building and approach the desk, Hamlin went smartly along to Chief Inspector Kelsey's office.

The Chief and Sergeant Lambert, their appetites by now restored, were making short work of a plate of ham sandwiches when the constable knocked at the door. The Chief bade him enter. He glanced up with inquiry as Hamlin came in.

The constable told him that Garbutt had just called in to make his statement. 'I thought I'd better let you know,' he added, 'in case you want to talk to him again.'

Kelsey was about to take another vast bite of his sandwich. He paused and gave Hamlin a sharp look. 'What's this about?'

Hamlin produced the newspaper, still folded into a compact square. He set it down in front of the Chief.

Kelsey looked down at it. Part of a City page, columns of prices, changes, yields. Here and there an inked query mark or circle, a tick, underscoring.

He put down his sandwich and picked up the paper, unfolded it, ran his eye over the rest of the City section. Government stocks, bonds, trusts, equities, interest rates. More inked markings.

Hamlin and Lambert watched in silence as he turned to the front page, looked at the heading. The paper was a quality national daily, yesterday's date. In the top right-hand corner was a scribbled name: Ferndale.

Hamlin explained how he had come by the paper. 'Conway was absolutely shattered when I saw him at the bungalow,' he enlarged. 'But there he was, an hour or two later, sitting at the table in the interview room as cool as a cucumber, marking the financial columns. I thought it worth a mention.'

'You thought right,' Kelsey said with energy. 'Bring Garbutt along here as soon as he's made his statement.'

When Garbutt arrived in the office a little later the Chief didn't show him the newspaper, didn't mention it. He asked Garbutt to cast his mind back to when he had picked Conway up at Oldmoor station the previous evening. Exactly what had Conway been carrying when he stepped off the train?

Garbutt closed his eyes in thought. 'He was wearing his overcoat, he was putting his gloves on. He had his briefcase under his arm. Nothing else.'

'Was he carrying a newspaper? Maybe he had one sticking out of his pocket?'

Garbutt pondered before shaking his head. 'No, he had no newspaper.'

'You're certain of that?'

'Quite certain. But there was a newspaper in the porch at Ferndale when we got there. It was lying on the bench. Conway picked it up and shoved it in his pocket while he got out his key. I could see by the way he looked at the paper he wasn't best pleased it was still there. He'd mentioned earlier it was always a bad sign. When Anna was feeling poorly she wouldn't get out of bed all day, she wouldn't bother to pick up the post or the newspaper.'

Kelsey took him back again in close detail over the time he had spent at Ferndale on Monday morning. At the end there could be no scintilla of doubt: Garbutt had both seen and spoken to Anna Conway. She had unquestionably been alive and well at seven-fifteen when Garbutt drove her husband to Oldmoor station.

When Garbutt had left, the Chief sat with his head lowered, his elbows resting on the desk, his fingers pressing into his temples. There was a short silence, then Sergeant Lambert said, 'Conway was alone in the interview room. No one to talk to, nothing to distract his thoughts. He may have been trying to take his mind off what had happened. Better than sitting staring into space, brooding.'

Kelsey made no response.

'Could be a hobby of his,' Lambert went on. 'Studying the markets. The way another man might do a crossword. Something to steady his nerves, calm himself down. He might not even really have been aware of what he was doing, it might just have been force of habit. He must have been in a dreadful state of mind, he could have gone over on to automatic pilot, fallen back on anything to keep his sanity.'

Kelsey raised his head and looked at him. 'The milk,' he said. It had still been outside the back door yesterday evening when they got to Ferndale. 'Make a note to get hold of the milkman. Find out what time he delivered yesterday at the bungalow. If he saw sight or sound of Anna. If he saw or heard anything or anyone in or around the bungalow.

If he noticed anything at all in any way out of the ordinary, anywhere in that neighbourhood.'

The street lamps were blossoming rose and gold in the gathering dusk as they left the police station to drive out to Ferndale.

In the darkling garden Conway was clearing up after his labours. He came over to greet them, tugged off his garden-ing gloves, removed his wellingtons outside the back door, pulled on an old pair of casual shoes. He led the way into the house.

Again he offered refreshments; this time Kelsey declined. 'But don't let us stop you having something yourself,' he added. Conway gave a brief headshake in reply.

He showed them into the sitting-room and sat them down. 'We'd like to ask a few more questions,' Kelsey said as Conway took his own seat. 'To fill in details, help to put us in the picture.' Conway gave a nod. 'How long have you worked for your present firm?' Kelsey asked.

'For Zodiac? Nearly eight months.'

'Where did you work before that?'

'I worked at Ackroyd's, in Northcott.' An industrial town, seventy miles away. 'It's a family firm, they make and supply loose covers.'

'Why did you leave Ackroyd's?'

'I was getting married. I needed more money, better prospects. Ackroyd's operate just in that one area, and all they do is loose covers. Zodiac are much bigger in every way.'

Kelsey switched tack. 'The situation with regard to your wife's family, not being able to contact them—would you mind if we took a look through your wife's things? Might come across something.'

'Not at all.' He gestured them towards the bedroom but made no attempt to accompany them. He leaned back in his chair with an air of profound fatigue.

The bedroom was clean and tidy, the double bed neatly

made. On either side of its head stood a polished wooden cabinet.

Kelsey set about the chest of drawers, the wardrobe, the dressing-table, while Lambert dealt with the bedside cabinets. The one on the right held some masculine oddments; he turned his attention to the cabinet on the left.

The drawer contained a few trifles: a nail file, handkerchief, hair grips.

He opened the cupboard below. On the shelf, a folded bedjacket, a fancy glass jar half filled with assorted pieces of confectionery. On the floor of the cupboard, two boxes: a beribboned chocolate box and a smaller, wooden box, encrusted with seashells, varnished over.

The shell box disclosed trinkets and costume jewellery. And two flower sprays, dried now and faded: a spray for a lady's corsage and a fern-backed carnation for a man's lapel.

Lambert lifted the lid of the chocolate box. Inside was an advertising brochure for Anna's cruise. He picked it up and glanced through it.

Underneath the brochure lay two strips of passport-type photographs. One strip, of two photographs, was of Anna; the other, a strip of three, was of Conway. In one photograph Conway wore a broad smile, the second was a little blurred, but the third was an excellent likeness, clear and unsmiling.

Over by the window the Chief was looking through the dressing-table. In the far corner of the bottom drawer, beneath an orderly pile of silky feminine underwear, ivory-white, trimmed with lace, his fingers encountered the outlines of something round and hard inside one of the pieces of clothing.

He drew out the garment and unfolded it. He saw that it wasn't an item of underwear but a drawstring bag, handmade from almost identical ivory-white, silky material, edged with a lace ruffle. It was beautifully sewn with tiny stitches.

He loosened the drawstring. Inside the bag were some folded papers, a small, round, gilt and enamel pillbox, a lady's handkerchief of finest lawn with entwined initials embroidered in one corner. A pair of ornamental hairslides for a child, exquisitely fashioned from tortoiseshell and silver, shaped like butterflies. And two withered flower sprays: a carnation for the lapel, an arrangement for the corsage.

He sprang open the lid of the pillbox, revealing a screw of pink tissue paper. He lifted it out on to his palm, fingered open the tissue. Inside was a platinum wedding ring, almost new.

He raised his head in recollection, looking back at yesterday evening, Anna lying in the bath. There had definitely been a wedding ring sunk into the waterlogged flesh of her left hand, third finger, he was certain of it.

He returned his attention to the contents of the bag. He withdrew the folded papers, opened them out. A yellowed cutting from a provincial newspaper, giving an account of a local amateur theatrical production, an inset photograph of a handsome, middle-aged woman. A caption underneath supplied her name: Mrs Norma Jefford. He looked again at the embroidered handkerchief. The entwined initials clearly N.J. Norma Jefford?

He unfolded the two remaining papers. A birth certificate in the shortened form, recording name, date, place of birth; no address, no names of parents. The name of the child: ANNA MARIE NEWBY.

The second paper was also a certificate. Recording a marriage some eighteen months ago in Ribbenford, a town fifty miles away, both parties giving Ribbenford addresses.

The bride: ANNA MARIE NEWBY, spinster. Occupation: waitress. Age: 18. The bridegroom: WALTER HENRY REARDON, bachelor. Occupation: retired plumber. Age: 61.

CHAPTER 7

In the sitting-room Conway appeared to have slipped into a doze. He stirred and opened his eyes at the sound of their return.

The Chief made no mention of anything they had come across in the bedroom and Conway asked no questions. He put a hand up to his mouth, suppressing a yawn. He shook his head to clear it, blinked his eyes wide open.

Kelsey asked in a casual manner if Conway could put his hand on a copy of his marriage certificate.

'Yes, of course.' Conway stood up and went to a bureau. He came back with the certificate and handed it over.

The Chief ran his eye over the details: DAVID MALCOLM CONWAY, bachelor, an address in Northcott. Occupation: sales representative. Age: 30. ANNA MARIE REARDON, widow, an address in Whitbourn, a town fifteen miles from Northcott. Occupation: housewife. Age: 19. The ceremony had taken place in Whitbourn.

The Chief read aloud the entry relating to Anna. As he spoke the word *widow* he permitted his voice to take on a note of surprise. He glanced inquiringly at Conway.

'That's right,' Conway confirmed.

'Did you know her first husband?'

Conway shook his head. 'I never met him. Anna was a widow when I met her. I didn't know her all that long before we were married.'

'Can you tell us anything about this first husband—Walter Reardon?'

Conway shook his head again. 'I'm afraid not, I know nothing at all about him. Anna never talked about him. I didn't press her, it seemed to upset her.'

'Do you know how or when Reardon died?'

Again he shook his head. 'All I know is that she'd been widowed about three months when I met her.'

'When did you meet her? And where?'

'I met her in Whitbourn, last November, almost a year ago now. I often went to Whitbourn on business when I worked at Ackroyd's. I was over there one morning, driving into the town, and I almost knocked Anna down. She stepped out into the road without any warning, not looking where she was going. I had to swerve to avoid her, I missed her by inches. She was pretty shaken. It shook me, too, I can tell you.

'I drove her home—she was living in a rented flat, not far away. She'd moved to Whitbourn after her husband died. I asked her if there was some friend or neighbour who could come in but she said there wasn't anyone.

'I made her some tea. She was still very shaky so I stayed and talked to her. I was concerned for her, she seemed so young to be widowed, all alone. I was in the town again a few days later and I called to see how she was. She'd got over her shock, she seemed pleased to see me. I asked her if she'd like to come out for a meal that evening, after I'd finished work.'

He spread his hands. 'We were married three months later. We moved here, into Ferndale, at the beginning of March. I'd already fixed myself up with the job at Zodiac, I started work there the week after we moved in here.'

'Did Anna have a job when you first met her?'

'She had a part-time job. She worked in a woolshop in the afternoons.'

'Was that her regular work? Shop assistant?'

'I don't think so. I know she worked in a café before she married Reardon, she mentioned it once. She did say the name of the café but I can't remember what it was.'

A brief silence descended on the room. Conway suddenly blurted out: 'I can't help feeling I'm to blame for Anna's death. I ought to have realized what was going on inside her head.'

His words came out in a rush. 'I should never have brought her to this house, it's far too lonely and isolated. Anna told me she wanted somewhere quiet and peaceful, in the countryside. I thought Ferndale would be ideal, but I see now it was no good at all for her. She'd never lived in the country, she had no idea what it would be like, on her own all day, with me out at work.

'I thought she'd soon make friends but she seemed to find that difficult. Then, when she wasn't well, she found it harder than ever, she couldn't face going out among strangers.'

His voice broke. 'I should never have allowed myself to be talked into persuading her to go away for a holiday on her own. I'll never forgive myself for that.' Tears glittered in his eyes. 'It was far too much to expect of her, I can see that now as clear as day, I can't understand how I could have been so blind to it before.'

He shook his head helplessly. 'One of the last things I said to her was about going shopping tomorrow afternoon. We were going to buy her clothes for the cruise.' His face was drained and haggard. 'The state she must have been in, that would have been just about the last straw.'

Eight o'clock on Wednesday morning found Chief Inspector Kelsey and Sergeant Lambert setting out for Whitbourn, a workaday town of no great size or beauty.

Anna's address in Whitbourn, at the time of her marriage to Conway, turned out to be the middle flat of three in a converted Edwardian house in a respectable suburb.

When repeated rings at the door of the flat produced no response they went down to the ground-floor flat, but they fared no better there. They mounted the stairs to the top flat and here they had better luck. A powerful smell of frying onions percolated out on to the landing; a radio played inside.

The sergeant's ring was answered by a cheerful, busy-looking old man wearing a brightly-coloured plastic apron, and clutching a fork. When the Chief identified himself the old man's face lit up at the prospect of a little excitement to enliven his day. He urged them inside—he must attend to his onions, he was preparing a casserole for his lunch.

He stood by the cooker, jabbing away at the contents of the frying-pan while Kelsey explained why they had called. Did he remember a young woman who had lived in the middle flat for some months, leaving there at the end of February? A Mrs Anna Reardon.

The old man shook his head with an air of deep regret. 'I'm afraid I can't help you there. I only moved in here at the beginning of June.' The middle flat was empty at present, it had been empty for the past two weeks. 'You'd better talk to Mrs Hudspeth,' he advised them. 'Down in the bottom flat.'

He began to chop a slab of beef into ragged cubes. 'She's lived here for years. She won't be home till well turned six, she's a supervisor at a discount store.' He made a face. 'Bit of a tartar, but decent enough. Divorced, lives here by herself.' He gave them directions for the store, on the outskirts of town.

'We won't bother with Mrs Hudspeth now,' Kelsey decided as they went down the stairs again and out to the car. 'We can catch her later.' Instead, they drove to Ribbenford, to the address shown for Walter Reardon at the time of his marriage to Anna.

Ribbenford was just such another town as Whitbourn, somewhat larger, equally busy, equally unremarkable. It took them some time to locate the house; it stood in a little rural enclave not yet invaded by the forces of progress. An attractive detached property, late Victorian, medium size, substantially built.

Kelsey looked up at it as he got out of the car. Worth a pretty penny these days. He knew at once there was no one at home: all the windows closed, not a sound to be heard. But Sergeant Lambert pressed the bell all the same. They went round to the back and tried again, expecting, and getting, no response. A long rear garden, sheltered and secluded; a tall hedge of mixed shrubs running the entire width of the garden, some yards from the house.

There was no near neighbour but the Chief remembered passing a newsagent's a few minutes back. They got into the car again.

The shop was doing a brisk trade; they waited outside for a lull. The young woman behind the counter gave them a friendly, inquiring glance as they came in.

The Chief revealed his identity. 'We're looking for some people by the name of Reardon,' he added. He mentioned the address. 'We've called at the house but there's no one at home. We wondered if you might know what time anyone's likely to be in.'

'There's no one by the name of Reardon living there now,' she told him. 'It's a young married couple there now, with kids. He'll be out at work. She was in here half an hour ago. She always calls in on Wednesday to pay the papers. She leaves the kids at the play-group and goes into town, shopping. She usually goes by again about half past twelve. I'm sure you'll find her at home around lunch-time.'

'There were Reardons living in the house before this young married couple moved in?' Kelsey asked.

'That's right. This couple bought the house from Mrs Reardon after her husband died last year.' She clicked her tongue. 'It was a dreadful business. I felt ever so sorry for poor Mrs Reardon, she was knocked sideways by it. She couldn't wait to sell up and clear out of the place. Couldn't blame her. Must have been a terrible shock, him dying in that horrible way.' She gave a little shudder. 'What a way to go.'

She looked up at Kelsey. 'Ever such a nice man, Mr Reardon. Always got his papers here. Never had much to say but always very polite, always a nice smile.'

She broke off as the door pinged before a fresh surge of trade.

*

At the Ribbenford police station luck was with them again: an inspector who had worked on the investigation into Walter Reardon's death was in the building and could spare them half an hour.

The inspector had had some acquaintance with the dead man; Reardon had been employed as a plumber by a firm of jobbing builders in the town and over the years had often worked at the house belonging to the inspector's parents. He had found Reardon an excellent tradesman, quiet and steady, with a pleasant manner.

'Reardon died August last year,' the inspector told them. 'He was found dead in his garden.' The autopsy revealed that he had died after ingesting a quantity of liquid weed-killer concentrate. The inquest returned a verdict of Misadventure; the court expressed sympathy for the widow.

The court had taken the view that Reardon was largely responsible for his own death. He was in no sense a toper and never frequented pubs but he had for many years been in the habit of brewing his own beer, putting up his brews in old lemonade bottles and the like. His main stock of homemade beer was down in the cellar but—according to a former workmate who had known him a long time—he always kept two or three bottles in the garden shed, to refresh himself while he worked.

But beer wasn't the only liquid kept in miscellaneous bottles in the shed. Reardon had, many years ago, like his father before him, belonged to a local gardening club whose members bought fertilizers, insecticides and the like in bulk at reduced prices, sharing the purchases out between them, most of them none too fussy about the containers they used.

'Asking for trouble,' the inspector said grimly. 'Decanting the stuff into any old bottle, sticking it away any old how in the shed. Hardly any labels and what there were you could barely read. Tins and boxes holding God knows what, piled up on the shelves. Reardon puts out his hand one fine day, picks up the wrong bottle, takes a good long swig—

and bingo! The coroner delivered a good old lecture about
it, I can tell you.'

'Any possibility of suicide?' Kelsey asked.

The inspector pulled down the corners of his mouth. 'No
indication of it, it was never seriously suggested. Reardon
had no sense of smell, he'd lost it after a bad cold years
before, never got it back again. That meant he hadn't much
sense of taste, either.' He flung out a hand. 'There was stuff
in that shed must have been there forty or fifty years, going
back to his father's day, some of it. Thick with dust, covered
in cobwebs. Beats me how he hadn't killed himself years
before.'

He grimaced. 'Boiling hot day, sun beating down. He
was violently sick a couple of times. The lower part of the
garden slopes down, the shed's right at the bottom. The
shed door was open, he'd managed to drag himself a few
yards up the slope. His fingernails were caked with earth
and grass. He must have died in agony. He was alone in
the place at the time.' He looked across at Kelsey. 'Not a
death many men would choose.'

He was silent for a moment. 'Didn't take him long to
die—one mercy, I suppose. His heart gave out. He'd had a
dicky heart for some time, he'd taken early retirement
because of it. He wouldn't have had many years to live in
any case. The pathologist told us he could have gone any
time, the way his heart was.'

'The amount of weedkiller he swallowed,' Kelsey asked.
'Was it a lethal dose?'

'I'll say it was. He was thirsty, he took a good long swig,
enough to kill an ox. A younger, fitter man would have
taken a lot longer to die, days even, but he'd have died in
the end, even if he'd been found right away and taken to
hospital. Reardon wasn't found for a couple of days.'

'How come? Why was he alone in the place? Where was
his wife?'

'She was in hospital. Minor surgery, some gynæcological
problem. She'd been on the waiting list some time, she'd

been given a few weeks' notice to go in. Reardon drove her
to the hospital on the Tuesday morning. He was due to
pick her up again on the Friday. It was understood between
them that he wouldn't be visiting her while she was in there,
he had a horror of hospitals, he never even set foot inside the
place when he drove her there. Some childhood operation,
tonsils or adenoids, put the frighteners on him for life. The
arrangement was he would ring the hospital morning and
evening to ask how she was.

'He phoned all right on the Tuesday evening and again
on the Wednesday morning, but he didn't ring Wednesday
evening or at all on the Thursday. Nor on the Friday
morning, to fix what time he'd be picking her up. She wasn't
worried until then. They'd only been married four or five
months, she didn't have much to go on about how he might
be expected to behave in those circumstances. She imagined
his hospital phobia had turned out too strong even to let
him phone. She didn't mind, she thought she understood.

'She did try to phone him herself from the hospital on the
Thursday evening but she got no reply. She thought he
was probably out in the garden, couldn't hear the phone.

'She tried again on the Friday morning but still couldn't
get any answer. That was when she really started to worry.
She rang a woman she knew who lived fairly close. A Mrs
Trigg, she'd worked with her before she married Reardon.
Sensible sort of woman. She asked Mrs Trigg if she'd pop
round to the house to see if there was anything wrong. Mrs
Trigg didn't like the sound of it. She went up the road to
her brother-in-law and asked him to go with her. They
found Reardon lying face down in the back garden. Difficult
to tell how long he'd been dead. The best estimate was
somewhere around the middle of the Wednesday morning.'

The Chief still wanted to pursue the possibility of suicide.
'Could he have been upset about his wife going into hospital?
If he had such a phobia about hospitals, maybe he'd be
inclined to worry far too much.'

The inspector shook his head with conviction. 'There was no suggestion at all that he was depressed over his wife going into hospital. He knew it was only for minor surgery, she'd be home in a few days, there was no risk to her. He was told on the Tuesday evening the operation had been done, it was successful. He was told on the Wednesday morning she was coming along fine.'

'He had no financial worries?'

'None at all. He was comfortably off, he had no debts. He owned the house—it came to him on the death of his mother.'

'How did his wife take it?'

'Very hard indeed. She was obviously fond of him. He was donkey's years older than her but you come across these couples, often seems to work out very well.'

'Did she know about the set-up in the shed? How careless he was?'

'She knew he brewed beer and kept it in the cellar but she had no idea he kept any in the shed. Or about his habit of drinking straight out of the bottle when he was in the garden—it was his old workmate told us that. She never touched any kind of alcohol herself.

'She'd never set foot in the shed. She had no idea of the way he kept the various garden chemicals. She wasn't a gardener, she left all that to him. He'd made it clear the shed was his domain.'

'Did Reardon live alone before he married her?'

'He lived with his mother. He was a dyed-in-the-wool bachelor, never had a lady friend. The father had been dead for years. The mother lived to a very good age, he was devoted to her, by all accounts. I imagine it was the mother's death made him think about finding himself a wife. He got married less than a year after she died. This neighbour, Mrs Trigg, she'd known the Reardons all her life and according to her the marriage was happy.

'And Reardon had talked it over with his doctor before he got married—on account of the state of his heart. The doctor warned him he could be taking a big risk, it could finish him off, marrying a young wife.'

He grimaced. 'It seems Reardon got quite upset at that. He told the doctor there was no question of anything of that kind. Companionship and affection, that was what they both wanted, nothing else.' He moved his shoulders. 'The doctor told him in that case he could see nothing against the marriage.

'According to the doctor, Mrs Reardon took very good care of her husband. If it hadn't been for the accident she'd probably have given him an extra year or two of life.'

He inclined his head. 'Nothing much in the way of looks, Mrs Reardon, and a bit on the highly strung side. But she struck me as a very genuine young woman. She was absolutely shattered by his death, no question of it. Had to be sedated. Eyes all swollen up with crying.'

'Was Reardon's life insured?'

'Only for a modest sum. A policy he'd taken out years before with a friendly society.'

'Did he leave a will?'

'Yes. He made one at the time of the marriage. Very straightforward, left everything to his wife. Even if he hadn't left a will she'd have inherited everything. There was no other dependant.'

Yellow sunlight gilded the gardens as Sergeant Lambert drew up outside Mrs Trigg's cottage. There was no one at home but a neighbour directed them to the Parkway Café where Mrs Trigg worked from eleven till six.

The café stood on the outskirts of town. Kelsey sought out the owner and disclosed his identity. They were taken through into an office. Kelsey said nothing about Anna's death, offered no explanation as to why he was asking questions about her.

The owner remembered Anna well: hardworking, reliable, punctual, always anxious to do her best, well liked by the customers. He hadn't personally engaged her; she was already working in the café when he bought the business three years ago. The previous owner had left the district.

The Chief asked if he might speak to Mrs Trigg; he understood she had been a friend of Anna's. A few minutes later Mrs Trigg came along to the office. In her early fifties; a good-natured face, a motherly air.

When she understood the object of the police visit her amiable look was at once replaced by an expression of sharp concern. 'Is Anna in some kind of trouble?' she asked. Kelsey told her gently that Anna was dead, sketching in briefest outline the circumstances of her death. Mrs Trigg bent her head and shed some painful tears.

'Poor girl,' she said when she had recovered herself. 'What an appalling thing to happen. And her poor husband, too.' She looked up at Kelsey.'I'm not surprised she married again, she was the sort always liked to have someone to lean on.'

Kelsey wanted to know how Anna had come to work at the Parkway.

'It was getting on for four years ago now that she came here,' Mrs Trigg told him. 'It was just after Christmas. We had a notice in the window, saying Waitress wanted. I spotted her standing outside one morning, reading the notice. She seemed very young and nervous. She kept reading the notice, biting her lips, hesitating. I smiled at her and that seemed to make up her mind.

'She came in and spoke to me. She said she had no experience but she'd work hard if she was given a chance. She was very nicely spoken, good manners, very neat and tidy—not like some of these girls you get these days, purple hair stuck up in spikes and God knows what, enough to frighten the customers.

'I put in a word for her with the boss we had then, I told him I'd show her the ropes. He gave her a week's trial and then he took her on properly.' Anna had found herself a cheap bedsitting-room in the neighbourhood.

The Chief asked if she knew how Anna had come to be in Ribbenford, looking in through the café window.

'I did ask her that once,' Mrs Trigg told him. 'She said it was pure chance. She'd got on the first coach that was leaving the bus station. It happened to be going to Ribbenford. She'd never heard of the place till then.'

She moved a hand. 'It was pretty plain she'd run away from home but she told me she was turned sixteen so I couldn't see she was breaking any law. She never told me where it was she came from or why she'd run away from there. I could see she wouldn't like being asked questions. She never talked about her family.'

Kelsey produced a blown-up print of the best of the three booth photographs of David Conway. He opened his mouth to ask if Mrs Trigg had ever seen the man but she forestalled him.

'I know him!' she exclaimed. She threw Kelsey a sharp glance. 'Is that Anna's second husband?'

Kelsey nodded.

'I knew there was something going on between them!' she declared. 'Though she would never let on.'

She stared down again at the photograph. 'Very pleasant young fellow, friendly way with him. Good-looking, too.' She glanced up. 'I suppose after she was widowed she got in touch with him again.' She puckered her brow. 'I'm trying to think if I ever knew his name. I don't believe I did.'

'Conway,' Kelsey supplied. 'David Conway.'

'No, then I never did know it,' she said. 'The name doesn't ring any bell. Poor man, he must be taking Anna's death very hard. Why ever did she want to go and kill herself? Was it depression?'

'That's what we're trying to find out,' Kelsey answered. 'We're talking to people who knew her.'

'It's more than twelve months since I laid eyes on her,' she pointed out. 'She's never been in touch with me.'

'But she did work here for more than two years. You seem to have known her as well as anyone.'

'Yes, I suppose that's true,' she conceded.

'How well did you know David Conway?'

'I can't say I really knew him,' she came back at once. 'I saw him here in the café a few times but I only spoke to him the once, that was the first day he came in. And that was only ordinary chat, the sort you'd make to any customer.'

Kelsey indicated the photograph. 'You're quite sure this is the same man?'

'Oh yes.' Her tone held complete certainty. 'I've a good memory for faces. He came in here, you might say he was blown in here, one day in January—'

'What January are we talking about?' Kelsey interrupted.

'January last year,' she answered promptly. 'Best part of two years ago now.'

'Two years ago?' Kelsey queried. 'You're certain of that?'

'Quite certain. No doubt about it at all.'

CHAPTER 8

Mrs Trigg cast her mind back to that stormy morning. 'It was a dreadful day, a proper blizzard blowing. It was getting on for lunch-time. There were hardly any customers in the café, on account of the weather. I was over by the door when he came in, the door flew right out of his hand in the wind. He was laughing and apologizing, stamping the snow off his shoes. He told me he was over here on business, he saw the lights of the café. He thought he'd stop for something hot, it looked so cheerful and inviting. I brushed the snow off his coat.

'One of the other waitresses, Norma, she served him. She's not in today, it's her day off. She's a chatty sort, she had a good old natter with him, trade being so slack. Walter Reardon—Anna's first husband, only of course she wasn't married to him then—he was having his dinner at another table. Anna was serving Walter, making a fuss of him the way she always did. I could see this young man, this Conway you say his name is, looking over at them—not that either of them noticed. He was taking quite an interest in the pair of them. I could see he was asking Norma about them and she was rattling on.

'I said to Norma afterwards: "What was all that about? You were having a good old chinwag with that customer. You were talking about Walter and Anna, weren't you?" She laughed and said: "Well, what of it? I was just being friendly, he was a nice young chap. We were just passing the time, a bit of gossip."'

She looked up at the Chief. 'Walter was very lonely after his mother died, he got very low in himself. He'd never had to do any cooking for himself, I was sure he wasn't eating properly. I said to him why didn't he come in here every day for his lunch, he could well afford it. And it would make a break for him. He had to take things easy, because of his heart. He just used to potter about the house and garden.'

She widened her eyes at Kelsey. 'He hadn't been coming in long before he started making a beeline for one of Anna's tables every day. It got to be quite a joke among us, pulling her leg about him. She just used to smile and pass it off.

'Then she started going round to his house at weekends, and then it got to be two or three evenings in the week, as well. Doing a bit of cooking for him, keeping the house looking nice.' She raised a hand. 'All very proper and above board. Walter was highly respectable, never a word against him of any kind. And Anna was never the free and easy type, she never had a boyfriend.'

'You said earlier you were sure something was going on between Anna and Conway. What made you think that?'

'Conway came into the café again quite soon, he came in three or four times close together. He never came in at lunch-time after that first day, it would always be around five, half past, he'd be one of the last customers before we closed. He always sat at one of Anna's tables. I could see she was very taken with him. It crossed my mind she could be meeting him in the evening.

'Then Conway stopped coming into the café but I was pretty sure from the way Anna was behaving she was still seeing him. She seemed very happy, she took a lot more care over her appearance. And she'd rush off the minute we closed, in the evenings. She hardly ever went round to Walter's any more.

'It went on like that for a few weeks and then I noticed her looking very down in the dumps. After a day or two she started going round to Walter's again, as much as before— more often, if anything. I was sure it must be all off with the young man.

'Then one morning, not long afterwards, she came into the café and told me she'd decided to marry Walter, it was all settled. They weren't going to wait, Walter being the age he was and his health not being too good, they were getting married as soon as it could be fixed. She said she was very fond of him, he was good and kind. It would be a fair exchange: she'd look after him and do her best to make him happy for the time he'd got left, and he'd give her security, a home of her own. She said that was very important to her. And it wasn't as if he had any relatives she'd be doing out of what he had to leave.

'One of the waitresses said to her, joking like: "If it doesn't work out, you can always divorce him and get half his money." Anna really flared up at that, she was quite upset. She said: "I'd never treat him like that. I don't believe in divorce. People should stick to their bargains and do their best for each other. When I say, 'To love and to cherish till death us do part,' that's exactly what I'll mean."'

She inclined her head. 'Walter wasn't at all bad-looking for his age. He was quite tall and well built. He had very nice brown eyes and he still had a good thick head of hair,

though it was going grey. And he was always well turned
out.'

She drew a long sigh. 'Poor Anna! She was in a dreadful
way over Walter's death, blaming herself. She should have
made it her business to look inside the shed, she would have
realized the risks he was running. She should have known
there was something terribly wrong when he never phoned
the hospital on the Wednesday evening.'

She shook her head. 'Everyone told her it would have
made no difference, he'd been dead hours by then. But that
didn't console her. She'd been prepared all along for him
to die of a heart attack. She'd imagined he would go suddenly, all in a moment, no pain or suffering. Or maybe one
morning he just wouldn't wake up, it would all be very
peaceful.'

She sighed and shook her head again. 'But to go in that
horrible way, all that pain and terror—she couldn't take
that.

'She couldn't bear to be in the house, she sold up as fast
as she could, furniture and all. Walter had some lovely old
pieces, came down to him from his grandparents. It was his
grandfather built the house, he was a master cabinet-maker.
And there was a beautiful collection of old china, quite
valuable, I believe. It belonged to Walter's mother, she'd
got it from her mother. It all went, the lot.

'Houses were fetching terrific prices just then, you could
sell anything the moment the board went up. Anna didn't
give me her new address. I could see what she was doing—
cutting loose from a painful part of her life, starting out
again somewhere new, the way she'd done before, when she
left home and landed up in Ribbenford. She didn't call
round to say goodbye before she left. I went by one morning
and saw a furniture van there, the new couple moving in.'

'Did you ever see any sign of David Conway after she
married Reardon?'

She looked startled, shocked. 'Good heavens, no! She
wasn't that type at all, to play around with another man

when she was married. She was far too open and innocent for games like that.'

She stopped suddenly and frowned. 'I'd forgotten that,' she said, half to herself. She looked up at Kelsey. 'Only a little thing, I don't know what made me remember it just then. It was that time when she was really down in the dumps, just before she started going round to Walter's house again. Walter came into the café as usual one lunch-time. Anna was coming through from the kitchen and she saw him standing with his back to her, hanging up his coat. She stood there, looking over at him. She didn't see me, I was to one side, clearing a table. It was the expression on her face, I saw it quite plainly. Very calm and cool, as if she was weighing things up.'

She stared back into that frozen moment. 'So grown-up and calculating. I'd never seen her look like that before, it gave me quite a shiver. I'd never have thought she was capable of it.

'Then Walter turned round and saw her. The look went in a flash. She smiled at him the way she always did, sweet and gentle, as if butter wouldn't melt in her mouth.'

Lambert drew up for the second time before the house where Reardon had lived. This time there was a front window open; squeals of childish laughter echoed from the back garden.

A harassed-looking young woman came hurrying to the door in answer to Lambert's ring. 'Yes?' She was already half turned back towards whatever chore they'd snatched her from.

Kelsey told her who he was and why he'd called.

'But it's more than twelve months since Mr Reardon died,' she protested on a baffled note. 'We've never had anyone from the police come wanting to take another look at the garden or the shed since we moved in here. Surely the whole thing's over and done with by this time?'

The Chief tendered one of the artfully vague explanations,

well seasoned with things half said, that he had long ago perfected for those situations—and they were many—when for any one of a dozen different reasons he preferred not to serve up the bald truth.

His spiel worked as well as ever. She held the door wide for them without further argument. 'You can come through this way.' She led them along a passage to the back door. Appetizing smells of cooking floated out from the kitchen.

She stepped outside with them into the bright sunshine. On the paved area a few yards away two small children pedalled furiously round on scarlet tricycles, shouting excitedly to each other. They glanced briefly round, smiled and waved, continued their swift circling and shouting.

'I won't come down with you, if you don't mind,' the woman said. 'I'm up to the eyes at the moment.' She made a deprecating face. 'I'm afraid that part of the garden's not very tidy, we haven't got round to it yet. You won't find anything in the shed now belonging to the Reardons. The whole house, shed and all, was cleared out before we moved in. It had been given a good sweep through, not so much as a used matchstick left.'

A thought struck her as they made to move off. 'You'll need the key to the shed.' She darted back inside. 'My husband fitted a good padlock on the shed door as soon as we moved in,' she told them when she came back. 'We didn't want any accidents happening to the children.'

'Was there no lock on the shed before?' Kelsey asked.

She shook her head. 'Just an old hasp and staple with a wooden peg tied on with twine.' Her fingers described the arrangement. 'We gave the shed a thorough scrub and airing, then my husband decorated it.' She went back to her chores.

The two men walked down the path, through a rustic gateway set in the belt of shrubs. They found themselves in a long, sloping stretch of garden sadly in need of attention.

The shed stood in the farthest corner, near the boundary wall, shaded by spreading branches. The interior was now scrupulously clean and tidy, everything conscientiously labelled, ranged along the shelves in orderly fashion.

Kelsey came out of the shed again and locked it behind him. He stood contemplating the shadowy expanses. This part of the garden was in no way overlooked. The property was bounded on three sides by a stout brick wall with a wooden door let into it on the lower boundary, close to the garden shed. The wooden door opened by means of a latch and had in addition recently been fitted top and bottom with sturdy bolts.

The Chief drew back the bolts and lifted the latch. He stepped out and found himself in a narrow alleyway running between the road on his left and a lane on his right.

Across the alley a tall, close-boarded fence marked the boundary of another property.

He stood gazing thoughtfully down the alley. A person might walk along it without fear of being seen from either property.

He stepped back inside the garden and bolted the door again. He said nothing to Lambert. They walked in silence back up to the house, no longer meriting so much as a passing glance from the two children, now squabbling fiercely over possession of a toy horse on wheels.

Kelsey tapped on the kitchen window and the woman came to the back door, drying her hands on a towel. He handed over the keys.

'Those bolts on the door leading into the alley,' Kelsey said. 'Was it your husband put them there?'

She nodded. 'There were no bolts on the door when we came, anyone could have opened it. I don't suppose it mattered much, that alleyway's hardly ever used. But my husband's not one for taking chances, he's very security-minded. Bolts and locks everywhere, windows as well.'

They went back to the car. 'Easy enough,' Kelsey observed, 'for someone to nip into the garden from the alleyway after dark, pop into the shed, switch a couple of bottles round. Someone aware of the set-up, the lay-out. Someone who could nip in beforehand, if necessary, take a look round, come back again at the right moment—when Reardon's going to be on his own for a few days.'

'Just as easy for someone to nip down to the shed from inside the house,' Lambert pointed out. 'Maybe Anna didn't fancy waiting two or three years for Reardon's heart to give out. She takes a stroll down the garden the evening before she's due to go into hospital, she slips into the shed, out of view of the house, switches the bottles. She sets off for the hospital next morning with the trap all nicely set, ready to be sprung. Leaving her free to marry again if she wishes. With plenty of money to buy a house anywhere she likes.'

After a snack lunch eaten in a lay-by they drove back to Whitbourn, to the discount supermarket where Mrs Hudspeth worked as a supervisor.

A vast, echoing store, grey and functional, strictly no frills. The manager was closeted in his den with a sharp-eyed sleuth from head office. He came briefly to his door and listened with a distracted air to what the Chief had to say.

'Yes, certainly,' he agreed when the Chief had finished, in overpowering haste to get back to the sleuth, no doubt at this very moment rooting about in his desk. 'You'll find Mrs Hudspeth's office up there.' He jabbed a finger into the distance, at a windowed protuberance jutting out above the crowded aisles.

'Tell her you've spoken to me. If she's not in her office, ask any of the girls. You can't miss Mrs Hudspeth.' His hands gestured an outline. 'Blonde lady, on the large side. Don't keep her from her job any longer than you can help.' He darted a manic glance at the throngs of shoppers. 'Only got to turn your back on that lot for five minutes and all hell breaks loose.'

Mrs Hudspeth wasn't in her eyrie but some little distance away, beside a checkout. Indeed a large lady; she wore a nylon overall cut on the lines of a tent. And a lady of some calibre, judging by the look of her. She had been summoned to referee a spirited altercation between a mulish checkout girl and a stroppy male customer over the price of a jar of mustard pickle.

The customer was in full spate, darting frequent glances of appeal at the queue behind him, in a fruitless attempt to drum up support. The shoppers stared resolutely into space, implacably neutral and unmoving.

The customer paused for breath and Mrs Hudspeth delivered herself of a few crisply relevant observations. All at once the customer perceived the deep hopelessness of his case. He caved in abruptly, paid up and took himself smartly off without another word. The checkout girl smiled in unsubtle triumph. The queue began to move again.

Mrs Hudspeth had all along plainly registered the nearby presence of two tall, silent, broad-shouldered men in dark suits. She turned now and sent a raking glance over the pair of them.

The Chief stepped forward and introduced himself in a discreet undertone. He moved quietly with her to one side, told her he believed she might be able to help them. They were making inquiries about a Mrs Reardon who had taken a flat a little over a year ago in the house where Mrs Hudspeth lived.

'That's right,' the supervisor confirmed. 'I remember Mrs Reardon.' She led them up to her office, invited them to sit down but didn't sit down herself. She stationed herself at the window to maintain a keen watch over the swarming aisles.

'Fire away!' she commanded. 'I'm listening.'

The Chief produced the photograph of David Conway. He went over to the window and asked her if she'd ever seen the man.

She glanced briefly down. 'Yes, I saw him several times.' No hesitation, no trace of doubt in her voice. She returned her gaze to the scene below. 'He used to come to the flat to see Mrs Reardon, he always stayed the night.'

'You're certain this is the same man? You didn't give him much of a look.'

She grinned. 'I gave him all the looking I need but I'll give him another if it makes you happy.' She bent a long, hard stare at the photograph. 'I'm absolutely certain,' she confirmed. 'That's the man that used to come to see Mrs Reardon. I spoke to him three or four times, I saw him quite close. He sometimes arrived about the time I get home in the evenings, and he sometimes went off in the morning around the same time as me. We'd exchange a few words. Pleasant enough guy. Not bad-looking. One evening I dropped my doorkey in the snow, he helped me find it.'

She thrust out her lips. 'I'm not mistaken, it was definitely the same man. You learn to look at folk in this job, you have to.' She gave a grim laugh. 'If I have a dust-up over a dicey cheque card I can guarantee you I'll know that punter again, even if he doesn't show his face inside the store again for five years.'

'Did you have much to do with Mrs Reardon?'

She shook her head. 'Very quiet young woman, very reserved. When she first moved in I tried to be friendly. I told her if there was anything she needed, anything she wanted to know, not to be afraid to ask. If she was on her own any evening and fancied coming out for a drink or a meal, just pop down and say so. But she never did. Polite enough, but made it very clear she preferred to keep herself to herself.'

She moved her powerful shoulders. 'No skin off my nose. It's a free country.' What's all this in aid of? her sharp eyes demanded. I'm an upholder of the law, same as yourself, you can tell me. But Kelsey didn't choose to respond to that. Instead he asked another question of his own.

'How long was she in the flat before this man showed up?'

'No time at all, he showed up before she ever moved in. He was with her the first time I saw her. The pair of them came round one evening with the agent, to view the flat. She took it on the spot. She moved in the next week. He drove her over the day she moved in, he stayed the night.'

CHAPTER 9

She was quite positive in her recollections. 'He used to come two or three times a week, and every weekend. One thing I did notice, they never seemed to go out together, not from what I ever saw. They always stopped in the flat.'

'Do you remember exactly when Mrs Reardon moved in?'

'The first of October,' she answered promptly.

'Did you ever see any other visitors while she was in the flat?'

'No, never, there was only ever the chap in your photo.'

Kelsey was struck by a sudden thought. 'Did you ever hear this man's name mentioned?'

She pondered before shaking her head. 'No, never. And Mrs Reardon didn't leave any address when she left the flat. I didn't know she was leaving or where she went.' She threw out a hand. 'Just vanished into thin air one day. I came home from work and it was all dark upstairs, not a sound. I knew for a fact there was still a month to go on her lease, so I had a word with the landlord. But he said it was all in order, she hadn't done a bunk, she'd paid the final month in full before she left.'

She looked reflective. 'There was never any mail came for her after she'd gone, not even junk mail.' She levelled a glance at the Chief. 'You're the very first person that's ever come asking about her.'

At a quarter to six Kelsey and Lambert drove out of the forecourt of the Cannonbridge police station, bound once again for Ferndale.

David Conway had got in from his day's work a few minutes before they reached the bungalow. He answered the door to them, still in his dark business suit. He showed no surprise, he looked listless and subdued.

They followed him into the sitting-room. His briefcase stood beside the open bureau. Papers were spread in orderly array on the desk flap. He asked if they'd like something to eat or drink. Kelsey declined but added, 'Don't let us stop you having something yourself. We can talk as you eat.'

Conway shook his head. 'I've already eaten. I stopped for something on the way home.' He sat them down and took his own seat facing them.

'That was an interesting little fairy story you told us yesterday evening, about how you met Anna,' Kelsey began briskly. 'One or two imaginative touches. Now I don't intend to waste your time and I hope you're not going to waste any more of mine. It may save you giving us another load of poppycock if I tell you we've spent a busy day and as a result we now know a good deal more of the true facts of your association with Anna.

'We've been over to Whitbourn and we've been over to Ribbenford. We've talked to the Ribbenford police, we've talked to Mrs Trigg at the Parkway Café and we've talked to Mrs Hudspeth—the woman in the flat below Anna, in Whitbourn. We know when and where you first met Anna. We know the circumstances of Anna's marriage to Reardon and we know the circumstances of Reardon's death. We know you helped Anna find the flat in Whitbourn and you helped her move into it. We know of your association with Anna all the time she was living in Whitbourn.'

Throughout this recital Conway sat relaxed. He appeared neither surprised nor disconcerted, his face wore a look of weary resignation.

When the Chief came to a full stop Conway gave a languid nod. He seemed still to be suffering a degree of shock, as if incapable for the time being of reacting strongly to anything at all.

'It wasn't that I had any wish to mislead you,' he said
flatly. 'I simply couldn't face going into the whole story
and I couldn't see that it was at all necessary. Just because
somebody dies, it doesn't mean you're entitled to know
every last little detail about that person's life.' His tone grew
livelier, stronger. 'Even a dead person must be entitled to
some privacy.'

He looked across at Kelsey. 'That time in Ribbenford
when Anna and I broke up, that was a very unhappy period
in my life. I did my best to forget it ever happened. It had
nothing to do with how she died. What difference does it
make, now that you know about it? It doesn't tell you
anything more about Anna's death and that's what you're
concerned with, surely? Anna's still dead. It doesn't bring
her back.'

He closed his eyes briefly. 'The very last thing Anna
would ever have wanted would be for me to be sitting here
talking to two total strangers about intimate details of her
life. She was a very private person.'

He gave Kelsey a direct, open glance. 'I didn't plan on
saying what I said to you yesterday about the way I met
Anna, it just came to me on the spur of the moment. I
thought if I said I met her accidentally in Whitbourn, you
need never know about her first marriage and the bargain
she made with Reardon. That wasn't something I liked
thinking about, let alone talking about to strangers.'

He gazed earnestly at the Chief. 'I couldn't have borne
you setting Anna down as mercenary and hard-headed,
trying to feather her nest from a cold-blooded marriage.'
He thrust out his hand. 'She wasn't like that at all. It was
just that she was so desperate for security, she seemed to
need that more than anything, and what security seemed to
mean to her first and foremost was a home of her own. I
believe it was the result of her childhood, whatever that
was.'

He paused. 'That business of nearly knocking her down
in the road—I didn't invent that. It did actually happen

and it happened around the time I told you it did, but of course I'd already met up with Anna again some time before then. It flashed into my mind when you asked me how I'd met Anna, that's how I happened to come out with it. It was when Anna was living in the flat in Whitbourn and I was seeing her regularly. I had to go over to Whitbourn unexpectedly one morning and I thought I'd look in and surprise Anna.

'I called at the flat but she'd already gone out to the shops. I drove off again and then I spotted her walking along in front of me. She suddenly turned without any warning and stepped out into the road. It gave us both a terrible fright, the car actually brushed her coat.'

'All that's as may be,' Kelsey said crisply. 'It's neither here nor there now. I've one or two questions to put to you now, and this time, if you've no objection, we'll have the truth, the whole truth, and nothing but the truth. We'd sooner not have to start talking about obstructing the police but it's as well to bear in mind that it's always a possibility.'

Conway smiled slightly and gave an acknowledging nod.

'To go back to the beginning of your association with Anna, you took up with her more or less immediately after you first met her in the café?'

'That's right. I very much wanted to marry her but the moment I mentioned marriage she asked me where we'd live if we did get married.' He grimaced. 'I didn't have much money. I said we could live in my flat in Northcott, to start with. It was only a one-bedroom bachelor affair, furnished, but it was all right, in quite a decent neighbourhood. We'd both be working, we could save every penny to put down for a deposit for a little flat of our own after a while, then, later on, a small house, a little terrace house, maybe, that we could do up. It's what a great many young couples do, it takes most people half a lifetime before they actually own a house. I thought it could be a lot of fun, something to work for, to do together.'

He flung out a hand. 'But she wasn't having any of that.

She was adamant she'd have to have a house right away—
and it had to be a decent house, not any poky little terrace
house. She didn't want to hear about mortgages or deposits
or scrimping and saving for years. And she didn't want to
hear about starting off in my bachelor flat. I was flabber-
gasted at how strongly she felt about it, it was like an
obsession with her.

'I was baffled how she could ever have imagined someone
like me, an ordinary sales rep, could possibly have had
enough money stashed away to buy a decent house outright.'

'Maybe she had an idea of her own to offer,' Kelsey
suggested in an expressionless tone. 'Maybe she said: "I've
got a much better plan—why don't I marry Walter Reardon? He can't last more than a year or two. It wouldn't
mean I'd have to stop seeing you. I could easily slip away
to meet you. Reardon wouldn't know anything about it and
what he wouldn't know wouldn't hurt him. It wouldn't stop
me looking after him properly, he'd still get his fair share
of the bargain. After he's dead I'll have his money. We can
get married, use the money to buy a house of our own."'

Conway heard this with increasing signs of distress. 'Good
God, no!' he exclaimed when Kelsey had finished. 'There
was never the slightest suggestion of anything like that! It's
a monstrous idea! Anna would never have dreamed up
anything so cold-blooded, she wasn't capable of it. And I
wouldn't have wanted to have anything to do with her if
she had come out with a plan like that.'

He gestured sharply. 'I knew you'd start judging her the
moment you heard about her marriage to Reardon. I knew
you'd see her as ruthless and grasping, that's why I never
said anything about it.' He shook his head helplessly. 'She
wasn't like that at all. You've got to believe me.'

'Were you on intimate terms with her before she decided
to marry Reardon?'

Conway made no attempt to equivocate. 'Yes, we were.'

'Did this intimacy continue during her marriage to Reardon?'

Conway half rose from his chair. 'It most certainly did not!' His tone was deeply agitated again. 'She'd never have behaved like that! Never in a million years! She was as straight as a die.' He sank back into his seat.

Kelsey pressed unswervingly on. 'Easy enough for her to phone you at your flat in the evening when Reardon was busy in the garden. Fix a time and place where you could pick her up in your car. I dare say you were often over Ribbenford way on business. All she need tell Reardon was she was off out to the shops, or going for a walk or calling in at the Parkway Café to have a natter with the girls, she'd be back in an hour or two. Reardon wouldn't raise any objection.'

Conway shook his head with force. 'There was never anything like that! Never! Never! Never! I'd never have dreamt of agreeing to anything like that when she was married to someone else. And Anna would have been horrified at the thought. She'd have thought it totally wrong and immoral, utterly dishonourable.' His face flamed. 'And so would I.'

There was a short pause. 'So,' Kelsey went imperturbably on, 'you told Anna you didn't have the money to buy a house. What happened then?'

Conway looked down at the floor. 'She said there was no point in us continuing. It would never lead anywhere, we'd better finish. But I couldn't give her up. I went round to her digs two or three times, I tried to get her to change her mind. Then one evening she came out with it: she'd decided to marry Reardon, they were getting married right away.' He put a hand up to his face.

'You'd known about Reardon all along?'

He nodded. 'I never actually met him or spoke to him but I saw him in the café the first time I went there. I only ever saw him once again after that, the day he married Anna.' He closed his eyes briefly. 'It was pretty plain to me that first day in the café that he was sweet on Anna and she didn't make any secret of it when I asked her about him. I couldn't take it very seriously then, it never crossed my mind for an instant that she could ever contemplate marrying him, he was old enough to be her grandfather.' Revulsion showed in his face.

'When she actually told me it was all settled, she was going to marry him, I simply couldn't believe it. I thought she was just saying it to hurt me, she was upset because I didn't have the money for a house. I was sure she'd soon get over that and begin to see reason. She'd realize the flat wasn't all that bad, it would do to start with. I was still certain she'd agree to marry me in the end.

'I still kept on going round to her digs. Every time I went I was positive this time she'd say yes, of course she'd marry me, she'd never been serious about marrying Reardon.'

His voice grew unsteady. 'But she never did say that. One evening she told me straight out I wasn't to go round there again, I must stop pestering her. She was one hundred per cent serious about marrying Reardon.'

He made a despairing gesture. 'What could I do? Not a damn thing. She went ahead and married him. I found out when the wedding was going to be. I went and stood in a doorway across the road from the register office. I watched them come out, with Mrs Trigg and one of the other waitresses from the café. None of them saw me. They were all smiling, looking happy.' His voice shook. 'I did my best to forget her.'

He looked across at Kelsey. 'There was no contact of any kind between us all the time she was married to Reardon.'

'Did you at any time go to Reardon's house?'

'Never during the time she was married to him. I only ever set foot in the place once and that was the day she left it, to go to the flat in Whitbourn. All I did then was drive up, go inside and pick up her cases.'

'Did you ever at any time go into the garden?'

'No, never at any time.'

'Perhaps you went into the garden on your own, after dark, maybe?' Kelsey persisted. 'Perhaps you slipped in from the bottom alleyway?'

'Why on earth would I want to do that?' Conway asked with astonished outrage.

Kelsey didn't answer that but fired another question. 'Did you ever go into the garden shed?'

'I could hardly go into the shed if I never set foot in the garden,' Conway retorted with increasing agitation.

'You haven't answered my question,' Kelsey pointed out implacably. 'I ask you again: Did you ever go into the garden shed?'

'Never at any time,' Conway replied with heat. 'I was never in the garden, I was never in the shed. I never even laid eyes on the shed. What are you trying to suggest?'

Kelsey made no answer to that. After a moment Conway's agitation appeared to subside as if he no longer had sufficient energy even to be able to keep his anger fuelled. He lapsed into an exhausted silence.

After a brief pause Kelsey began afresh with undiminished vigour. 'So, Anna married Reardon. When did you next get in touch with her?'

'I never got in touch with her, it was she who got in touch with me,' Conway replied in a tone of marked languor. 'I would never have tried to contact her again. I considered the whole thing over and done with the day I watched her come out of the register office. Then she phoned me one evening at my flat. It was about the middle of September, around six months after she'd got married. She told me about Reardon's death, about the inquest and the verdict. I was knocked back, I hadn't known anything about it.

'She sounded in a pretty poor state. She said she was selling the house, she wanted to get away as soon as possible. She was looking for somewhere temporary till she decided what she was going to do. She said she'd very much like to see me again, she was badly in need of a friend.'

He moved his head. 'Of course I said I'd go over. I'd never been able to get her out of my head. She told me not to come to the house, it might set tongues wagging locally. We fixed where to meet. I helped her find a flat. I ran her about in the evenings and at the weekend, looking at places. When she found one that would do I drove her over the day she moved in.'

'Why did she pick on Whitbourn?'

'She didn't particularly choose it. She just wanted somewhere far enough from Ribbenford where no one knew her and she could put it all behind her. We looked at flats in two or three other towns, it just happened that the first suitable one was in Whitbourn.'

'Did she talk much about Reardon's death?'

'She never talked of it at all after that first time when she told me about it over the phone, and she'd said little enough about it then, only the bare facts. That was always her way, she never would talk about anything that really upset her.'

Another silence followed. 'When we were here yesterday,' the Chief said at last, 'we didn't see any bank books belonging to your wife.'

Conway dragged himself to his feet. 'You could have seen them if you'd asked. It never crossed my mind. Anna kept them with mine, in the bureau.' He went over and unlocked a drawer. He produced a number of items, among them a building society account book, a cheque-book, bank statements, a post office savings book.

Kelsey cast his eye over them. Some pretty substantial sums. All in Anna's name. 'Is there any joint account?' he asked.

Conway shook his head. 'We never had any joint account, it was never suggested.' He gave Kelsey a direct look. 'I never touched a penny of Anna's money, never wanted to. If we had found a house it wouldn't have been owned jointly, the deeds would have been in her name alone.'

'Did she have any investments? Stocks and shares, bonds, unit or investment trusts?'

Again Conway shook his head. 'She never had anything like that. What you see there is the total of what she had. I did try, I tried several times, to get her to invest some of the money, not just leave it sitting there, barely keeping pace with inflation. I tried to explain she had more than enough to buy the sort of house she was looking for, enough to furnish it, too.

'And she wouldn't need to pay the full purchase price outright. It would make good business sense to take out the maximum mortgage she was allowed. That would leave her a good sum to invest in various ways. I tried to explain how she could spread the risk, how her capital would be almost certain to grow substantially over the years.' He shook his head. 'I could never even begin to persuade her. She would never even consider a mortgage. She was absolutely adamant; the money had to be instantly available, all of it, ready for when the right house turned up, to pay out the whole purchase price.'

He blew out a long breath. 'I never gave up trying to persuade her. I used to mark suitable investments for her, I kept on showing them to her. It became a kind of hobby with me, I got very interested in the City pages. But I could never get her even remotely interested.'

He stared back into days that were gone. 'She always looked so frail and vulnerable but she had a backbone of steel. You could never get her to budge an inch once she'd made up her mind about something.'

He stopped abruptly. He looked over at Kelsey and suddenly burst out: 'It still hasn't properly got through to me. I can't get it into my head she's really gone. It's like a terrible dream, I keep thinking I'll wake up. I'll be walking up the path to the front door and she'll be there, smiling at me, throwing her arms round my neck.' He dropped his head into his hands, his shoulders shook with racking sobs.

Later, as they got into the car again, Lambert said: 'Conway's mighty anxious to protect Anna's good name. I don't know that I'm totally sold on this touching picture of her as a frail little innocent. It's my belief she was having it off with Conway all the time she was married to Reardon. Conway would never admit it now, not if he was to be hanged, drawn and quartered, he'd never allow himself to sully her precious image.' He set the car in motion. 'Good job adultery's not a criminal offence in this country. They'd be building a new gaol every three months.'

Kelsey made no reply but stared out through the windscreen in brooding silence.

'Then again,' Lambert conceded in the tone of one determined at all costs to be scrupulously fair, 'I suppose Conway could just be telling the truth. There might never have been any contact between them while she was married to Reardon.'

They reached a junction and he headed back for Cannonbridge. 'It's possible Anna played a lone hand from start to finish. She could have made up her mind to marry Reardon for his money from the very first moment she realized it was on the cards, long before she ever set eyes on Conway. Could be at that time she did honestly intend to look after Reardon till his heart gave out in the natural course of events.

'Then Conway appears on the scene. She falls for him, loses interest in Reardon. Then she discovers Conway has no money. She takes another look at Reardon, a very different look this time. This time she's not thinking of waiting for nature to take its course. She's in love with Conway, she's never been in love before. She's afraid to keep Conway waiting too long, he gets about a lot in his work, he might easily meet someone else.

'Now she intends giving nature a helping hand with Reardon—but Conway must never know anything about it, must never even begin to suspect what she's got in mind or she'll never see hair or hide of Conway again.

'If she is going to marry Reardon she'd better look sharp about it. His dicky heart might snuff him out at any moment before she's got his ring on her finger and not one penny of his money would come her way. So she marries him in a hurry, works out her plan to dispose of him, takes the first good opportunity—her summons to hospital—to carry it out. As soon as she decently can afterwards, she phones Conway. He comes running. The poor sap's absolutely innocent. He never knew or suspected anything about it from first to last.'

The lights of Cannonbridge ran towards them, glittering gold and amber in the darkness. 'After she's married Conway and they're living in Ferndale,' Lambert went on, 'it all begins to prey on her mind. Maybe Conway starts asking awkward questions about Reardon's death, maybe she catches him pondering, wondering, maybe he starts looking at her in a way she doesn't relish. Her nerves begin to get the better of her. There isn't a soul she can turn to, no one she dare confide in. She feels absolutely alone, a very long way from the good life she murdered Reardon for.

'One day it all gets too much for her, she comes to the end of the road. She takes a good slug of pills to calm herself, runs a bath, gets out the penknife. She steps into the bath and slits her wrists.'

CHAPTER 10

On Thursday morning Lambert contacted the milkman who delivered out at Ferndale. It seemed his times of delivery varied somewhat, according to the traffic, the weather, the day of the week. Mrs Conway usually left an indicator out with the empty bottles, showing how much milk was required that day. He sometimes caught sight of her about the house or garden and he always saw her on a Friday, when she settled up with him. She was invariably polite but never in the least talkative.

On Monday morning he had left the milk, as usual, by the back door. He had seen nothing of Mrs Conway, nor of any other person. He had seen no car or other vehicle, no pedestrian, anywhere in the vicinity of the bungalow. In fact he had noticed nothing in any way out of the ordinary. The time of his call, to the best of his recollection, had been around nine-thirty.

Lambert asked if he had heard any sound from inside the
bungalow, but he couldn't really say. He had certainly
heard no loud or unusual noise, he would have remembered
that. But as for the ordinary sounds of normal activity, he
had no recollection; he wouldn't expect to register such
sounds.

Shortly after noon Kelsey and Lambert set off for Harvington, the town shown on the birth certificate they had found
at Ferndale as the place where Anna Marie Newby had
been born very nearly twenty years ago.

The eight-year-old newspaper cutting they had discovered in the same drawstring bag had been taken from
the local Harvington newspaper. It appeared from the cutting that Mrs Norma Jefford, the handsome, middle-aged
woman whose photograph adorned the column, was the
widow of a prominent local businessman and a leading light
in amateur theatrical circles in the town.

On this fine sunny day Harvington appeared a pleasant
enough place with an air of solid prosperity. They had no
difficulty in finding the theatre mentioned in the column; it
stood close to the town centre. The foyer clock showed
two-thirty as they pushed open the swing doors.

Kelsey asked the woman in the box office if she knew Mrs
Jefford. He didn't explain who he was.

The woman's face lit up with a smile of affectionate
admiration. Everyone connected with the Harvington
theatre knew Mrs Jefford. Production, fund-raising, pub-
licity—not many local theatrical pies Mrs Jefford didn't
have a finger in. She lived now in a luxury flat in a nearby
mansion block. 'But she may not be in,' the woman warned.
'She gets about a good deal.'

But Mrs Jefford was at home. She was on her knees in
her sumptuously furnished sitting-room, sorting with little
cries of pleasure through a trunkful of nineteen-twenties
evening gowns and accessories, a totally unexpected dona-
tion to theatre wardrobe, brought to her door twenty

minutes ago by a young man, a regular theatregoer. His grandmother had recently died at an advanced age and he had been charged with the disposal of her personal possessions.

Mrs Jefford reverently withdrew each item from its tissue wrappings: beaded dresses, embroidered shawls, lace scarves. More riches below: gloves, fans, satin shoes, hair ornaments. She laid them carefully out on the thick-piled carpet.

The ring of the doorbell pierced her absorption. She rose reluctantly to her feet. Still a striking-looking woman, slim and graceful, immaculately groomed, casually elegant. Dark hair touched now with white, pale skin still fine and smooth, eyes of a brilliant sapphire blue.

An aura of expensive perfume found its way to the Chief's nostrils as she opened the door. He declared his identity and apologized for disturbing her. He asked if she was acquainted with a young woman by the name of Anna Marie Newby.

Her eyes flashed wide open in alarm. 'Anna?' she cried. 'Has something happened to her? She's my granddaughter.'

'May we come in?' Kelsey asked. 'I'm afraid we bring bad news.'

She turned without a word and led the way into the sitting-room. She sank into a chair, oblivious of the glittering treasures arrayed on the carpet.

Kelsey took a seat nearby. He told her gently that Anna was dead. She began to weep in a heartbroken fashion.

Lambert went into the kitchen to make tea. By the time he returned she had regained control and was dabbing at her eyes.

The tea began to revive her. 'Was it an accident?' she asked.

Kelsey looked at her with compassion. 'No, it wasn't an accident.' He waited for a moment to let that fact sink in before adding, 'She was found dead in her bath, with her wrists cut.'

She gave an appalled gasp and broke again into tears. When she had recovered she said with great sadness, 'I suppose suicide was always on the cards.'

'Why do you say that?' Kelsey asked.

'I'm afraid she didn't have a very happy childhood. She suffered a great deal.' She looked up at him. 'Did she leave any letter?'

'No, there was no letter. Her doctor had been treating her for anxiety and depression.' She gave a nod at that as if to say: That doesn't surprise me.

She had last seen Anna nearly four years ago; she had never heard from her during that time. She was astonished to learn that Anna had been twice married. Kelsey sketched in brief details of her life since leaving home; Mrs Jefford broke in from time to time with questions. He went on to explain that Anna would never speak about her family or background, they had only been able to find Mrs Jefford because of the newspaper item.

She looked down at the cutting with tears in her eyes. 'Fancy her keeping that all those years!' She glanced suddenly up. 'Her parents—they won't know she's dead?'

'I'm afraid not. Do they live in Harvington?'

She shook her head. She explained that Anna's parents had divorced when Anna was four years old. They had both remarried, both had new families. Anna's mother, now Mrs Lowther, lived ten miles away; Anna's father, Adrian Newby, seven miles in another direction.

'Would you break the news to them?' she asked with appeal. 'I don't think I could—'

'You can leave it to us,' Kelsey assured her. 'We'll speak to both parents.'

She closed her eyes in relief. 'I'm afraid I never see anything of Adrian Newby, or any of his family, these days, not since the divorce.' She drew a sighing breath. 'I do see my daughter but only very occasionally. Louise, her name is, she's my only child.' She faltered. 'There have been difficulties between us for a long time—over her first marriage, to Adrian Newby.'

The Chief asked if she felt up to telling them about Anna's childhood, the reasons why she had left home.

'I see that you have to know,' she told him. 'I'd rather it was me you heard it from, I'll give you the unvarnished truth.' Her eyes filled with pain. 'I did precious little for Anna while she was alive. The least I can do for the poor child now is to set the record straight.'

She didn't wait for questions but launched into a flow of words, with brief pauses and occasional tears. As if, Kelsey thought, she had never been able to pour it all out freely before to anyone, and it was a relief at last to be able to unburden herself.

Her daughter Louise had become pregnant when she was barely sixteen. Her boyfriend, Adrian Newby, was a year older, the son of a local estate agent. Adrian was still at school, Louise at a secretarial college. They were not in love; neither had the slightest wish to marry.

The Newby parents and the young couple were strongly in favour of an abortion but Louise's father, a devoutly religious man, rigidly set his face against the idea. He would settle only for marriage.

Mrs Jefford's eyes strayed to a photograph in a heavy silver frame; clearly her late husband. An impressive countenance, strong and resolute; an unsmiling, penetrating gaze.

Mrs Jefford had nursed grave doubts about the wisdom of forcing a marriage. The young couple were very immature, not in the least suited. But—at this point in her story she broke down again—she had never seriously opposed her husband in the matter. He was considerably older, she had always deferred to his judgement. The most she had done was to suggest that Louise should have the baby and then give it up for adoption, leaving the youngsters free to continue their education untrammelled. But her husband rejected this proposal as strongly as he had rejected abortion.

Marriage alone would satisfy him. In the end he bore down all opposition.

The young couple were hastily married and set up in a flat. Adrian abandoned all idea of a university, left school and went into the family business.

It was scarcely surprising that the marriage failed. The young couple were bitterly unhappy. They fought from the start like trapped animals.

Mrs Jefford clasped her hands tightly. 'From the day Anna was born I don't think she ever had a moment's love from either of her parents.' She was treated with persistent coldness and unkindness, unrelenting aversion. 'Though I don't think either of them ever actually laid a finger on her,' Mrs Jefford added in trembling tones. Anna was never a pretty baby. She seemed all skin and bone, she cried constantly.

Louise, now fiercely and unremittingly hostile to her mother, made it blisteringly plain her help and advice weren't wanted. 'She blamed me for not standing up to my husband,' Mrs Jefford said in unsteady tones. 'She never forgave me.'

Her knuckles showed white. 'My husband died, very suddenly, when Anna was about three years old.' Her voice was harsh with old grief. 'Louise had scarcely spoken to him since the wedding. The whole business poisoned the last few years of his life. I'm sure it helped to kill him.'

The following year Louise and Adrian were divorced. 'Neither of them wanted to keep the child.' Her face was ravaged. 'Adrian tried to renounce all right to Anna but Louise forced him into joint custody.'

After they had both remarried Anna was shunted from one family to the other, an outsider in both, wanted in neither, a reminder of things they'd all rather forget.

Her voice shook with suppressed tears. 'And of course the younger children took their tone from their parents.' Anna was always the scapegoat, the butt. Never complaining, never understanding what it was she had done to deserve such treatment. Always trying to please, to placate, hungry for any crumb of affection.

'As soon as she was old enough she was packed off to boarding-school.' It was made clear to Mrs Jefford that she wasn't to visit or write to her at the school. 'I was permitted to see her sometimes during the holidays, when she stayed with Louise. I was never allowed to see her alone.'

Tears shone from her eyes. 'I believe she was fond of me. I'd given her a pair of tortoiseshell hairslides once, when she was about five years old, I'd come across them in an antique shop. I noticed whenever I saw her she was always wearing them, even when she was in her teens.'

'She still had them,' the Chief told her gently. 'We found them among her things.'

A month or two after Anna turned sixteen it was Louise's turn to have her for the Christmas holidays. Anna was supposed to be staying on at school till the end of the summer term, it hadn't been decided what to do with her after that; she hadn't done well at school.

Mrs Jefford jerked her hand. 'She ran away soon after Christmas. She took some clothes and what bit of money she had and went off very early one morning without a word, before anyone in the house was up.

'I wasn't allowed to know about it till months later. I was devastated. It was far too late by then to do anything about it. None of them had made the slightest effort to find her. The truth was they were all relieved, the last thing any of them wanted was for her to turn up again. As far as I know, none of them ever heard from her again.'

Before they left she gave the Chief the addresses of Anna's parents. 'And you'd better have the address of the place where Louise works,' she added. 'She won't be home yet. She's the manageress of a bridal wear shop.'

'The inquest's tomorrow morning,' Kelsey told her as she came with them to the door. 'I don't know if you'd—' But she was already shaking her head.

'I'm afraid I couldn't face that.' She was visibly hanging
on to self-control.

But she did wish to attend the funeral. Kelsey promised
to let her know when it would take place.

The door closed behind them and they went off along the
corridor. Kelsey knew with certainty that she would already
have collapsed into a passion of weeping.

CHAPTER 11

Half an hour's drive brought Kelsey and Lambert to the
town where Louise lived. The bridal wear shop occupied a
prime site in one of the main streets. A Thursday afternoon
towards the end of October was possibly not a peak time for
choosing wedding finery but trade appeared brisk enough.

The premises were bright and airy, elegantly furnished,
the merchandise beautifully displayed. A subtle perfume of
lily-of-the-valley scented the air. Against the background of
pearly silks and alabaster satins, ivory georgettes and frosty
laces, the two big men in their dark suits stood out like a
pair of grounded crows in a snowy garden.

Mrs Lowther was talking to a customer by the fitting-
room. She cast an arrowy glance at the alien intruders. She
lost no time in excusing herself, handing over the customer
to an assistant, moving across with smooth speed to deal
with them. She was her mother's daughter in slenderness
of figure, dark hair and brilliant blue eyes, but her strongly
moulded nose and uncompromising chin had clearly come
to her from her father. She had an air of restless, driving
energy.

Kelsey employed his most discreet tone in revealing his
identity; he asked if he might speak to her privately. She
had a word with a member of staff before taking them
along to a room, part office, part kitchenette. She glanced
pointedly at her watch as they all sat down.

'I'm afraid we bring bad news,' Kelsey began. She froze. 'It concerns your daughter Anna.' She let out a sigh, her shoulders relaxed. 'I'm very sorry to have to tell you she's dead.' She lowered her head and closed her eyes. He saw plainly that it was in relief; she had feared for one terrible moment that it might be her husband or one of her other children.

Kelsey went on to say that they had just come from Harvington where he had broken the news to Mrs Jefford. He added a word to explain how it had come about that they had spoken to Mrs Jefford first.

She raised her head. Her eyes, bright as jewels, stared into his. 'How did she die?'

The answer left Kelsey's lips with unusual bluntness. 'She was found dead in her bath. Her wrists had been cut.'

Mrs Lowther uttered a smothered sound and sprang to her feet. She ran out through a door into a cloakroom. They heard the sound of violent retching.

Lambert's eye had already located an electric kettle. By the time Mrs Lowther came unsteadily back, pale and shaken, he was fishing beakers from a cupboard, milk from a fridge. She sank in silence into her seat, not looking at them.

As she drank her tea her colour gradually returned. The Chief began to dole out, piece by piece, the information he had already given Mrs Jefford. He was at no point prompted by any question from Mrs Lowther. She didn't ask how Anna had fared after leaving home, if she had fallen into danger or hardship. She expressed no flicker of surprise at the mention of the two marriages. She didn't ask if the marriages had been happy, how the first had ended. Nor did she ask if Anna had left any letter before she stepped into the bath.

When he had finished, the Chief asked if she had had any contact with Anna in the last four years. In reply she gave him two words: 'No, none.'

He experienced throughout a sense of being on the receiving end of a powerful, unspoken shaft of command, directing him to finish what he had to say and clear out. As if she was determined to admit into her mind not one single unnecessary shred of knowledge, to provide not the slightest foundation for later brooding, for lying sleepless in coming dawns. It was plain how Anna had come by her tendency to suppress unwelcome thoughts, drive down unpleasant facts.

'The inquest is being held tomorrow,' Kelsey informed Mrs Lowther. 'I don't know if you would wish—'

She gave an immediate, vigorous shake of her head, still in silence.

'It's up to the coroner when the body is released for burial,' Kelsey added. 'I dare say it will be released tomorrow. There's no need for you to decide now if you want to attend the funeral. We can let you know the date, or you could get in touch with Mr Conway—' But she was already rejecting the suggestion with another vigorous shake of her head.

As they rose to leave she suddenly found her tongue. 'Have you told Adrian yet? Anna's father?'

'Not yet,' Kelsey answered. 'We're on our way there now.'

She opened a drawer and took out a comb and some cosmetics. She crossed to a wall mirror and attended to her face and hair.

'You're sure you're all right?' the Chief asked.

'Yes, thank you,' she answered with composure. 'I'm perfectly all right.'

Their eyes met in the mirror. 'I can see what you're thinking,' she told him coolly as she turned to put away her toilet things. 'I've no doubt you've heard the whole story— with knobs on—from my beloved mama.' She flicked her fingers over her shoulders, the front of her elegant suit, chasing specks of powder. 'Am I in the least sorry that Anna's dead? That's what you're thinking, isn't it?' He made no response. 'I'm not going to stand here and pretend something I don't feel,' she pursued in the same relentless tone. 'For your information, the answer is: No, I can't say I'm in any way sorry.' She looked him full in the face. 'I'm only sorry she was ever born.'

She led the way back into the airy salon. 'Thank you for taking the trouble to come and see me.' Her tone was formal, a hostess bidding goodbye.

She didn't walk with them to the door but at once resumed her duties. Kelsey turned on the threshold and looked back. She had come to a halt by a stand of frothy, virginal gowns. Beside her, a slender blonde and her plump mother were earnestly outlining their requirements. Mrs Lowther listened with her head inclined, an expression of rapt attention, her lips curved in a professional smile. She was back in business.

'She's a strange one,' Sergeant Lambert said with distaste as they went back to the car. 'She's put it all behind her in an instant.'

'I don't know that she'll find it as easy as she hopes to shrug off poor Anna,' Kelsey observed. He didn't envy Mrs Lowther her state of mind when she woke in those small dark hours. She couldn't pack Anna off to boarding-school now. Or send her to stay with her father. Anna might prove to be a ghost that would take some laying.

The Newbys lived on a small upmarket estate reared in recent times on two adjacent stretches of land known locally from time immemorial as Jacob's Bottom and Pollard's Piece. The developers, in search of greater refinement, had sought to exorcise the taint of rural uncouthness by christening the streets and roads after royal residences.

Shortly after five-thirty Lambert turned the car out of Sandringham Way, along Balmoral Rise and into Windsor Close. He drove in through the handsome gates of the Newby residence and saw a silver BMW drawn up by the entrance. The lights were on in the house. A man was walking up the front steps.

At the sound of their wheels the man halted and glanced round. As he started back down the steps the front door swung open and a woman appeared in the oblong of light. The man turned his head to speak to her. She remained where she was, looking across at them. The man continued on his way towards them.

The two policemen got out of their car and went to meet him. 'Mr Adrian Newby?' Kelsey asked.

He nodded. He was tall and well built. In the waning light he appeared good-looking enough. He had a relaxed manner, an air of unflappable self-possession.

Kelsey introduced himself and saw at once by the change in Newby's expression that he had taken them for prospective clients.

'I'm afraid we bring bad news,' Kelsey said for the third time that day. 'May we come inside?'

'Yes, of course.' Newby turned and went swiftly ahead to where his wife stood in the doorway; he said something to her.

The two policemen came up the steps and Newby introduced his wife. Blonde and blue-eyed, with regular features; she would have been very pretty fifteen years ago.

Newby took them inside and closed the door. In the light of the hall Kelsey could see in him a distinct resemblance to Anna, the same light brown colour of hair, the same set of the eyes.

The house was spacious, attractively designed and decorated; it spoke unmistakably of money. The sound of young voices drifted into the hall from a room along the passage.

'I'll just have a word with the children,' Mrs Newby said. 'They're having their tea.' She went rapidly off.

Newby showed them into a long sitting-room and indicated seats. Mrs Newby came back almost at once. By this time husband and wife were prepared for almost anything Kelsey might have to tell them. They fixed their eyes on his countenance.

'It concerns your daughter Anna,' the Chief began. And saw apprehension lessen at once in both faces.

'I'm very sorry to have to tell you she's dead,' he added. On both faces a further lessening of apprehension, a look almost of relief. Both expressions rearranged an instant later to display appropriate concern. They're extraordinarily well matched, Sergeant Lambert thought, like two halves of a whole.

'Dead?' Newby repeated like a man querying some minor detail in an invoice. 'How did it happen?'

'She was found dead in her bath with her wrists cut,' Kelsey told him with a sensation as of repeating lines in a play. Mrs Newby uttered a muted sound of shocked distaste.

Newby frowned. 'Damnfool thing to do.' His tone displayed nothing so much as mild irritation. 'What did she want to go and do that for?' He stood up and went over to a drinks table. He glanced an invitation at the Chief, who shook his head in reply. Newby poured Scotch for himself and his wife.

'She was being treated for depression,' the Chief enlarged.

Newby grimaced at the word, accepting without need for further probing the modern curse and its consequences. He resumed his seat.

Once again the Chief found himself meting out the same gobbets of information, adding that he had already broken the news separately to Mrs Jefford and Mrs Lowther.

Newby heard him out with no marked show of interest. 'I hope old man Jefford's satisfied now, wherever he is,' he commented when the Chief had finished. 'And Mrs Jefford—interfering busybody.' His tone held echoes of ancient rancour. He fell silent for a moment. 'I must say, though, I wouldn't altogether have believed it of Anna.' He looked reflective. 'I never thought I'd hear of her again. I certainly never imagined this is what I'd hear.' He might have been idly remarking on some chance paragraph come upon in a newspaper.

Kelsey looked inquiry at him.

'I'd have given her credit for more backbone,' Newby
amplified. 'She always looked as if she couldn't swat a fly
but underneath I always thought she was as tough as old
boots.' He moved his head judicially as if delivering a final
verdict. 'Yes, on the whole, I must say I'm surprised.'

He looked Kelsey full in the eye. 'We always did our best
for her. We sent her to a good boarding-school. Cost us a
fortune, I can tell you.'

He sought no information about the life Anna had lived
after fleeing Harvington. But one question he did fire off as
though struck by a sudden invigorating thought.

'This first husband of Anna's—what sort of chap was
he?' His manner now showed keen interest.

'He was a great deal older than your daughter,' Kelsey
answered.

'A widower?'

'No, a bachelor.'

'Well-to-do?'

'Comfortably off, as far as I know.'

'Did he own a house?'

'Yes.'

Newby leaned forward. His eyes gleamed. 'A decent
house? Some character to it? Good-size garden? Have you
seen the property? Could you put a figure on it?'

'Yes, I have seen the house,' Kelsey replied when Newby
paused for breath. 'It looked a good enough property to me
but I'm not up in the housing market, I certainly couldn't
put a figure on it. It passed to your daughter, if that's what
you want to know.'

Newby gave a nod of satisfaction and then smartly fired
off another round of questions. 'This bungalow she was
living in with the second husband—was that Anna's property? Or owned together with the second husband, do you
know? Owned jointly or in common? Does it carry any
mortgage? Any mortgage protection policy?'

Kelsey strove to keep his tone even. 'The bungalow is
rented, furnished.'

Newby looked disappointed, but not excessively so, as if he hadn't entertained any great hopes of the bungalow. 'I'd better have the name and address of the second husband,' he said briskly. He took out a pocket diary and noted the details in a businesslike fashion. 'I don't imagine Anna left a will, not at her age. There are strict rules for intestacy, as I'm sure you know. Where there are no children, as in this case, the parents are entitled to some portion—'

'Your daughter did leave a will,' Kelsey cut in in tones of ice.

That brought Newby's head sharply up.

'Very straightforward, I understand,' the Chief added. 'She left everything to her husband.'

Newby sat back with a punctured air. After a moment he looked openly at his watch. 'Is there anything else?' he inquired. 'We're meeting a client and his wife, taking them out to dinner. We'll have to be thinking about changing, we can't be late.'

Before Kelsey could open his mouth to reply, the phone rang in the hall. Newby excused himself and went out to answer it.

Mrs Newby looked across at Kelsey. 'I can't say I'm surprised that Anna took her own life. I always thought her very nervy. She was never a happy child.' She turned down the corners of her mouth. 'The children never liked her. She never fitted in. The atmosphere always changed when she came to stay—and not for the better. She was a very silent child. You could never tell what she was thinking. You'd catch a look in her eyes sometimes, it'd give you the shivers.'

Newby came back into the room. He didn't close the door, didn't sit down again but remained standing by the threshold. Again he consulted his watch.

Kelsey got to his feet. 'The inquest will be held tomorrow morning, if you think of attending,' he said. 'Eleven o'clock. It shouldn't take long. It'll be opened and adjourned, resumed later.'

Newby gave a decisive shake of his head. 'I won't be there tomorrow, or when it's resumed. I've no wish to attend, I've nothing to contribute.' He didn't ask to be informed in due course of the inquest findings.

Did he wish to be informed of the date of the funeral?

No, he did not. He was kept very busy, he couldn't possibly get away.

Anna's ghost isn't likely to trouble him much, Kelsey thought as he got into the car. Or his lady wife.

'It's small wonder Anna was fond of Reardon,' he said as Lambert switched on the engine. 'She'd have been grateful to anyone who gave her a kind word. Anyone who loved her.'

CHAPTER 12

In an age of ever-increasing violence, carnage on the roads, disasters of every kind, the death of Anna Marie Conway warranted not one syllable of mention in any national newspaper and no more than a brief paragraph tucked away in a corner of the local weekly and evening papers.

Anna had lived for only a few months in a scattered community, she had mixed locally to a minimal extent; scarcely anyone in the area had been aware of her existence. The inquest, like her death, aroused barely a flicker of interest.

Friday morning blew in wild and stormy. By eleven o'clock rain lashed the windows of the Cannonbridge court house, keeping away the idle and the curious.

The proceedings were as brief and formal as the Chief had indicated. The Coroner released the body for burial.

Afterwards Kelsey walked with David Conway to the car park. Conway was hardly in the mood for conversation. He looked heavy-eyed and lethargic, though his manner was composed. He told the Chief he was going straight off about his daily business; he found it best to maintain as normal a routine as possible.

Bright and early on Monday morning Chief Inspector Kelsey came striding into the police station. At the sound of his feet slapping smartly down along the corridor, Sergeant Lambert pricked up his ears. Here we go again, he told himself with philosophic resignation, charging off down another road.

The precise direction of that road soon revealed itself. 'That firm in Northcott,' Kelsey said. 'Where David Conway worked before he went to Zodiac—'

'Ackroyd's,' Lambert supplied.

'That's the one. We'll nip over there as soon as maybe. Have a ferret round.'

But it was turned one o'clock before they managed to get away, almost three-thirty by the time they reached Northcott. The town was humming with activity even at this hour on a Monday afternoon.

They went first to the address Conway had given on his marriage certificate but they got no joy there. The flat was one of four in a converted turn-of-the-century house in a respectable district. Only one of the four flats produced a tenant in response to Lambert's rings on the doorbells: a young woman who had moved in only a month before. She knew nothing of the other tenants or of any previous occupant of her flat. She had never heard of Conway.

They went next in search of Ackroyd's. They found the workshops and offices in a side street some distance from the main shopping centre. Nothing fancy about the premises. A solid, down-to-earth set-up; an air of well-founded prosperity.

Mrs Ackroyd, a Junoesque woman in late middle age with a lined face and vigilant eye, was bustling about, overseeing every aspect of production. Her piled-up mass of steel-grey hair made her look even taller than she was, the padded shoulders of her jacket, even broader. Her husband was at work in his office. A few stones lighter, a few inches shorter and a few years older than his good lady; a quiet, stoop-shouldered man with a reflective cast to his countenance.

A girl took the two policemen along to Mr Ackroyd's office. Mrs Ackroyd had sailed in a few moments before to ask her husband the details of some order.

Kelsey introduced himself and indicated that he would like to ask some questions about a Mr David Conway who had worked for them until eight months ago.

'That's right,' Mrs Ackroyd confirmed at once. 'He left us in February to go to Zodiac Soft Furnishings.' She didn't invite them to sit down. 'Why are you asking questions about him?' A belligerent gleam appeared in her eye. 'You're not trying to tell us he's been mixed up in something shady? I'll never believe that.'

'We're not trying to tell you anything,' the Chief said patiently. 'To the best of our knowledge Mr Conway hasn't put a foot wrong.' He launched with practised agility into one of his soft-soap spiels designed to cast dust into the eyes as much as to enlighten.

It worked well enough with Mrs Ackroyd but Sergeant Lambert fancied he perceived a certain sardonic scepticism lingering in her husband's gaze, though Ackroyd made no comment, merely assuring the Chief they would both be happy to assist in any way they could.

Mrs Ackroyd unbent sufficiently to ask them to sit down but she didn't go so far as to produce tea or coffee. She didn't take a conventional seat herself but perched on the edge of her husband's desk, dominating the confined space with her substantial presence and commanding eye.

Ackroyd consulted his records: Conway had worked for the firm a little over three years. He had come to them with an excellent reference from a furnishing store called Dorrell's, in a town at a fair distance from Northcott. He had left Ackroyd's for Zodiac solely in order to better himself. There had been no disagreement or unpleasantness of any kind; they had been very sorry to see him go.

He had given them first-class service, had been one of their best salesmen, very popular with the customers. He had worked exclusively on house calls. 'Most of our domestic customers are women,' Ackroyd enlarged. 'They always liked Conway. Good listener, sympathetic manner. Big asset in this business, a manner like that. But it's got to come naturally, it never works if it's false, just put on to sell the goods. And it came naturally to Conway.'

'Funny thing, though,' Mrs Ackroyd put in. 'For all the women liked Conway so much, he wasn't really interested in women himself, you can always tell.' She waved a hand. 'He wasn't gay or anything of that sort, just not very interested in women. A young man like that, good-looking in that boyish way, soft-hearted with it, he's the sort women throw themselves at. I was always surprised some female hadn't snapped him up. I used to tell him: You're a natural born victim for some neurotic bloodsucker that'll hang on like a leech, given half a chance. Don't say you haven't been warned.'

She gave a hoot of laughter. 'You remember the way Joyce Kimbolt used to behave?' she reminded her husband.

'Indeed I do.' Ackroyd grinned. 'Joyce took a real shine to Conway,' he told Kelsey. 'Forever ringing up, leaving messages. Would he go round and check the fit of the new covers? Did he think the material was showing signs of fading? Any old excuse. I used to pull his leg. I used to tell him: You want to get in there. She'll come in for a packet one day, even if she is turned forty with a face like a doorknocker.'

Mrs Ackroyd gave a cackling laugh. 'She'd have had a damned good try at catching him, too, if it hadn't been for her dad. Jack Kimbolt would never have let a sales rep marry his daughter. With Joyce's looks it could only be the money he was after.'

'Coal merchant, Jack Kimbolt,' Ackroyd enlarged.

'Started out in a back street, humping coal. Worked like a horse, never took a holiday, never thought of retiring. Built up a wonderful business, put his profits to good use, too, very shrewd investor.' He grimaced. 'Fell down dead coming out of the pub six months ago. Joyce came into every penny—only child, mother been dead ten years.'

'Joyce got shut of the business as soon as she could,' his wife chipped in. 'She never liked it. Not genteel enough for her taste, too dirty and messy.' She uttered a snort of contempt. 'Not that she could have run it anyway. She wouldn't have known where to begin, she'd have gone bust inside twelve months. She has as much notion of business as a babe in arms. Never done a day's work in her life.'

Lambert slid a glance at the Chief and saw unmistakable signs of restlessness.

'She put the house up for sale as well,' Ackroyd added. 'I don't know if she's managed to sell it yet.'

The Chief pushed back his chair. 'Thank you for sparing us your time,' he was beginning when the phone rang on the desk. Kelsey rose swiftly to his feet. 'We won't keep you any longer,' he said rapidly as Ackroyd lifted the receiver. 'We'll find our own way out.'

Ninety minutes' solid driving took them to the market town where Dorrell's old-established furniture store occupied a good position in the central shopping area.

The street lights shone in the deepening dusk, the store was on the point of closing for the day. The manager wasn't best pleased to be detained at this hour. He dealt with them expeditiously, didn't waste time asking questions of his own.

Yes, he remembered David Conway well. He had joined Dorrell's from Bredon House, a high-class department store in Graysholt, a fair-sized town over in the next county; he had come with first-class references. He had given excellent service, had never been in any kind of trouble during his two years at Dorrell's. He had lived in a modest bedsit, neither drank nor smoked. Quiet, courteous, obliging, liked by the customers. And scrupulously honest.

Why had he left?

The manager shrugged. 'Young single men on the way up, you can't hang on to them for long. He got restless, shut up inside the store all day. He went after a job where he could have some independence, get out and about. And Ackroyd's pay very good rates of commission, he could push his earnings up to a very good figure if he worked hard. And he certainly was a worker.'

He walked with them to the door. 'The thing I remember most about Conway,' he said as he let them out, 'was his nose for a customer. He could always tell the ones he could talk into splashing out on more than they'd bargained for when they came in.' He grinned. 'Don't know how he did it, but he was always spot on.'

Bredon House was an imposing Edwardian edifice dominating the High Street in Graysholt. Three o'clock on Tuesday afternoon saw Chief Inspector Kelsey talking to the store's personnel manager.

Yes, the records showed a David Conway. He had started work at Bredon House eleven years ago at the age of twenty. Before that—after leaving school four years earlier—he had worked for the Biddulphs, customers of Bredon House since its earliest days. Conway had brought a glowing reference from Miss Biddulph.

He had given every satisfaction during the five and a half years he had stayed at Bredon House. He had worked in various departments before settling down in Soft Furnishings.

Would the Chief Inspector like to have a word with Mr Freeth, head salesman of that department?

The Chief Inspector would.

Mr Freeth was deferentially conducting a grand dowager of a customer across to the lifts when the two policemen approached his department. They stood discreetly aside until the dowager had soared aloft, then the Chief stepped forward and engaged the head salesman's eye.

Freeth was a meticulously groomed gentleman with greying temples and a toothbrush moustache. He glided noiselessly towards them over the thick-piled carpet.

He took them into his office but before he would answer a single question they had first to satisfy him that nothing was going forward that might in any way compromise the good name of the store. It apparently never even occurred to him that there might be any question of Conway's good name suffering, he seemed to take it for granted that if anything untowards had been afoot, Conway could have had no hand in it.

'A very sensible young fellow,' he told them. 'Head well screwed on. Quick on the uptake, never needed to be shown anything twice. Very likeable personality. He had a flair for this kind of work, a good eye for colour and design. You've either got it or you haven't, you can't be taught it and you can't pick it up as you go along. Conway had it. And he always took a keen interest, that's more than half the battle.'

Conway hadn't been in the department long before he was sent out to customers' houses, handling special orders. 'He had a flair for that, too, dealing with customers. Some of them can be very difficult.' He smiled. 'He had a look, like a young man that could play a good game of cricket, every mother's favourite son—the ladies always liked that.' He gave a decisive nod. 'He'd have done very well here if he'd stayed. No doubt of it.'

'Why did he leave?' Kelsey asked.

Freeth's smiling expression turned to one of compassion. 'He wanted to get right away, he thought a complete change might help him. Very understandable in the circumstances. He was in a pretty low state, hardly surprising after what happened. He was dreadfully upset.'

He shook his head and sighed. 'It was after the death of his wife. It had been a terrible shock. He was devoted to her.'

CHAPTER 13

Kelsey's head jerked back. 'His wife?' he echoed. 'How long had he been married?'

'Only a matter of months. He got married without a word to any of us. Very understandable—she was a lot older than him, best part of twenty years, at a guess, I dare say there'd have been remarks passed.' He thrust out his lips. 'I must admit I was surprised when he got married, I'd have thought he was more the bachelor type. He never had a girlfriend on the staff here, not like some of our young men, keeping two or three on the go at the same time.'

'Did you know his wife?'

'Only very slightly, as a customer. She didn't come in all that often. Willett, her name was, Mrs Ida Willett. Pleasant enough to speak to. Timid, gentle sort of woman, quite nice-looking. Conway met her when he went to her flat from the store, about an order.'

'How did she die?'

'Misadventure, the inquest found.' Freeth grimaced. 'Usual tale: drink and pills.'

The main Graysholt police station, large and busy, wasn't far from Bredon House. An inspector who had dealt with the death of Ida Conway was present in the building, up to the eyes in a tricky case of his own but willing to take time out to talk to them.

It was almost six years since Ida's death and he refreshed his memory from the files.

A kind of death only too common nowadays; he had felt very sorry for the husband. Ida had a chronic drinking problem and her doctor had entertained good hopes of this second marriage, the steadying effect of the care and companionship of a loving and supportive husband—a husband, furthermore, who never touched a drop himself.

A straightforward enough case, according to the inspector. Ida had died on a Friday. A popular member of the Bredon House staff had reached retirement that day and a farewell party had been arranged for six-thirty in the staff canteen. For staff members only; no spouses or outside guests. Conway had gone to work in the morning as usual, had stayed on for the party, had been visible throughout, had remained till the end.

He reached home around ten-forty-five and found his wife dead, stretched out on the sofa in the living-room with an empty whisky bottle and a container of pills, three-quarters full, on the table beside her.

The pills were painkillers prescribed by her doctor for chronic low back pain. She well knew the correct dose and she also knew the pills must never be taken with alcohol. She had been using them without mishap for more than a year. There was no letter.

She had been dead for several hours when Conway found her. The police doctor put the time of death in the early afternoon. The post-mortem confirmed this opinion. She hadn't ingested an exceptionally large quantity of pills; it was the combination of pills and alcohol that had killed her.

There were two other flats in the house, one occupied by a young man, the other by a middle-aged married couple. None of them could throw any light on what had happened. All three had been out at work all day, the young man not returning home till half an hour after Conway had made his grim discovery. The married couple had returned home from work around six and had gone out again an hour later to spend the evening with friends; they had got back at midnight. So far as any of the three could tell, the Conways had got on well together, they had never heard raised voices or slamming doors.

Ida's doctor told the police she had been his patient for some four years. She wasn't a local woman, she had moved to Graysholt after a divorce from her first husband. She had

had a drinking problem for many years, long before moving to Graysholt, though she had improved appreciably in this respect since her remarriage. On her last visit to him, three weeks earlier, she had seemed in good spirits. She had spoken with warmth of the love and understanding of her husband.

There had been no insurance policy on Ida's life; she had made no will. As there were no children and no close relatives, everything went to her second husband, under the rules of intestacy. It was no great fortune, consisting chiefly of the modest flat and its run-of-the-mill contents, together with the remnants of the lump sum Ida had received in her divorce settlement.

Ida's first husband, Gregory Willett, had remarried shortly after the divorce. He was a successful businessman, still living in the town where he and Ida had lived throughout their marriage; he was an active and well respected local councillor.

He told the police he had had no contact with Ida since the divorce; he was very sorry to hear of her death. He would admittedly be better off by the sum of money he would no longer be paying Ida every month. This was not alimony—alimony had ceased in the normal way on Ida's remarriage—but an additional voluntary allowance he had made her from the time of the divorce and had continued to pay her after her remarriage. The payment of this allowance had by no means weighed heavily on him, he was certainly not in any kind of financial difficulty. His movements on the day of Ida's death were clearly and unequivocally accounted for.

'But that line of inquiry wasn't much more than a matter of form,' the inspector told them. 'There was never the slightest suggestion that Willett was in any way involved in Ida's death. The question was: Misadventure or suicide? We could find nothing positive to indicate suicide. Neither could the coroner. So, Misadventure it was.'

A silence descended on the room. Sergeant Lambert

glanced at the Chief. He fancied he could guess what the Chief was thinking: Never mind about Willett, what about Conway? Could he have helped Ida on her way? Lambert could without difficulty envisage two or three different ways in which Conway could have had a hand in Ida's death. And none of the other tenants had been in the house when Conway returned; he could have taken his time to alter the scene, falsify the evidence, add or subtract any item he thought necessary, before picking up the phone to ring the doctor, the police.

He saw hesitation in the Chief's face and again he fancied he could guess what the Chief was thinking: Never a good idea to stroll into a strange police station and blithely suggest to an officer that he might have missed something vital in an apparently open and shut case.

When the Chief did at last break the silence it was to voice not one but two queries—with a seemly air of diffidence. His first question was precise enough: had Conway left Bredon House at any time that Friday? To go out on a special order, perhaps? But the inspector couldn't recall raising that point with Conway, nor could he discover any record in the files of any such question having ever been asked.

Kelsey's second question was couched in less specific terms: had the police thought it at all possible that Conway might by some means or other have tricked Ida into drinking—all unsuspecting—the lethal combination of alcohol and painkillers?

The inspector's amiable expression vanished abruptly. 'We didn't think so.' His tone was decidedly frosty. He gave no sign of any wish to enlarge. After a moment he proffered a question of his own: 'This death you're looking into now, Conway's second wife, have you anything concrete against Conway? Anything to suggest her death wasn't suicide?'

The Chief shook his head.

The inspector moved his shoulders. There you are then, the shrug plainly said, easy enough to harbour fanciful suspicions about any sudden death, even easier to begin believing one's own imaginings. Doesn't necessarily follow they have any basis in reality.

Kelsey didn't need it spelling out when he'd reached the end of a particular road. He pushed back his chair and in the same instant the inspector also rose to his feet.

'I don't know what you make of Conway,' the inspector said in a tone grown affable again, 'but he struck me as the type that can't help attracting women with problems.' He moved his head. 'It's quite possible this second wife of his would have finished herself off sooner or later, whoever she was married to—or if she'd never got married at all.'

He stepped out into the corridor with them. Kelsey thanked him for his help. 'I wouldn't mind betting,' the inspector prophesied cheerfully, 'when Conway's had time to get over this lot, he'll go and do precisely the same thing all over again, let himself get lumbered with another female cut out of exactly the same cloth. Men like Conway never learn, they will keep on seeing themselves as knights in shining armour riding to the rescue of damsels in distress.' He shook his head. 'And God knows, there's never any shortage of helpless, mixed-up females, looking for Sir Gala-had.'

Promptly on the dot of five Gregory Willett, businessman, left his office and drove the half-mile to party headquarters for the surgery he held there on Tuesdays—a convenient time for folk to call in on their way home from work.

As he walked in through the door he instantly assumed the mantle of Councillor Willett, philanthropist, tireless fund-raiser for local charities, ready to grapple with the assorted problems of the residents of his ward.

A fair sprinkling of callers this evening. He dealt with them efficiently and expeditiously but always with a due meed of sympathetic care and solicitous attention. He had dispatched the bulk of them by the time Chief Inspector Kelsey ran him to earth. When the last client had taken himself off the two policemen went into the room where

Willett sat behind a table with a female party worker at his side.

Willett greeted them with a professional smile, rose to his feet and extended a hand in greeting; he invited them cordially to sit down. He was a tall, strongly built man, beginning now to run to fat. A dark grey business suit cut by a first-class tailor. In his mid-fifties, undoubtedly, in spite of the expert haircut striving to knock twenty years off his age. At the end of the working day he still exuded an air of pronounced vigour.

The Chief told Willett who they were and Willett at once jumped to the conclusion that their visit had to do with council business. The Chief swiftly disabused him of the notion and asked if they might talk to him in private, the matter was a personal one. The woman rose without a word and left the room.

'It's to do with the death of your first wife, Ida Willett—Ida Conway as she was at the time of her death,' Kelsey began without further preamble as soon as the door had closed again. Willett's expression altered sharply. 'I won't beat about the bush,' Kelsey continued crisply. 'I'd appreciate a straight answer to a straight question. The verdict on your ex-wife's death: Misadventure. Were you totally satisfied with that verdict?'

Willett regarded him in horrified astonishment. 'Ida's been dead going on for six years now,' he protested. 'What on earth are you raking it all up again now for?'

Thought raced behind his eyes. 'It's that cousin of Ida's, isn't it?' he suddenly burst out. He thumped the table. 'I knew he'd try to make trouble for me one way or another but I never thought he'd stoop to this. He's had it in for me ever since he lost the council contract back in the spring. That is it, isn't it? It is him that's been talking to you?'

He got to his feet and began to pace the room, his hands clasped behind his back, frowning down at the floor. His wheelings sent a waft of expensive after-shave about the confined space.

'Were you satisfied with the verdict?' Kelsey repeated.

Willett halted abruptly. He frowned down at the Chief. 'You believe now her death could have been suicide. That's it, isn't it? That cousin of hers has talked you into it. He hadn't been near Ida for years before she died, now all of a sudden he knows every little why and wherefore of her death.'

He craned forward, his hands resting on the table top. He fixed the Chief with his eye. 'He doesn't give a tinker's cuss for Ida or how she died, all he's out for is to get his own back on me. You must see that.'

His tone grew ever more earnest. 'I'm up for president of the Rotary next year, up for Mayor the year after. Could even be a knighthood in it for me one day. Not impossible if I keep my nose clean, play my cards right. If there's another investigation into Ida's death after all this time and it all comes out, her drinking, the details of the divorce—'

He sank into his chair. 'If they put me in the box the local rag'll have a field day. I could kiss goodbye to the women's vote for a start. If you lose that these days you might as well pack up and go home.'

He suddenly sat up, spying a ray of hope. 'But you can't overturn a coroner's verdict, can you? Once it's given, that's the end of it, surely?'

'I ask you again,' Kelsey said with unflagging patience. 'Were you satisfied with the verdict?'

Willett gave a long noisy sigh and collapsed into himself. 'How can I possibly say what happened? I wasn't there, I hadn't laid eyes on her for years. The verdict seemed right enough to me. I went over to Graysholt and sat in the court. I took my solicitor with me. He was satisfied with everything.'

He raked the two policemen with his eye. 'I'm going to level with you. You're not local men with some axe of your own to grind in all this. Ida was a hopeless drunk, she'd been boozing for years, long before we were ever divorced. That's the main reason I divorced her, there's only so much a man can stand of that sort of thing, in the end it's sink or swim. I had no choice, she'd have dragged me down with her.'

He grimaced. 'I felt very sorry for that second husband of hers, young Conway, getting lumbered with her. He must have gone into that marriage like a lamb to the slaughter. Very decent young chap, he struck me, very good to Ida by all accounts, very cut up about it all.' He waved a hand. 'Admitted, he came into a bob or two after she died, but I didn't grudge him that. I reckon he'd earned every penny of it.'

He darted a sharp look at Kelsey. 'You'll be doing Conway no kindness, stirring it all up again—you realize that?'

He spread his hands. 'It was always on the cards she'd die the way she did, sooner or later. Women in that state, tanked up to the eyeballs, who's to know what's in their minds when they pick up a bottle of pills? Doubt if they even know themselves.'

His voice took on a powerful note of appeal. 'What can it possibly matter now to anyone whether she killed herself on purpose or by mistake? It's a waste of public money going over it all again. Can't you let the poor devil rest in peace?'

He broke off abruptly and glanced at his watch. He uttered a groan as he saw the time. 'I've got to get home and change. I've got a function, very important, I've got to be there on time.'

Kelsey rose to his feet. Willett walked with them to the door. 'I'm throwing myself on your mercy.' His eyes looked desperate. 'I've slaved my guts out for this town. Don't destroy all that.'

He plunged a hand into his breast pocket and snatched out a wallet, pulled out a coloured photograph of a family group. 'My wife and sons.' He thrust the photograph under the Chief's nose. A handsome woman, young enough, by the look of her, to be Willett's daughter. Two sturdy young boys, one on either side of their mother, all three smiling into the camera.

'Think of them if you won't think of me.' Under the light Willett's brow glistened with a fine dew of sweat. 'Can't you let sleeping dogs lie?'

Kelsey let all that go without response. But he did vouchsafe one parting observation. 'This person you keep on mentioning, this cousin of your first wife—you might like to know I've never met the gentleman. I've never heard of him before this evening, let alone spoken to him.'

Willett's jaw dropped. He stood staring after them, openmouthed, as Kelsey stepped out into the corridor and went off towards the exit with Lambert following.

CHAPTER 14

Kelsey consulted his watch as they got back into the car. It would be turned eight by the time they reached Cannonbridge; another half or three-quarters of an hour wouldn't signify much. 'We'll look in on Conway on the way back,' he instructed Lambert.

The evening was fine and mild. As they drove through the town they passed excited groups of children garbed in witches' costumes and other fanciful gear, carrying pumpkin lanterns, on their way to Hallowe'en parties, trick or treat forays.

Conway was in the sitting-room, watching television, when Sergeant Lambert pressed the doorbell. He expressed no surprise at the sight of them, didn't ask why they'd called. He stepped aside to allow them to enter, closed the door and stood waiting for Kelsey to explain his errand.

The Chief came straight to the point. 'I'd like to take another look at your marriage certificate to Anna,' he said briskly.

Conway turned without a word and led the way to the

sitting-room. He went over and switched off the television. He produced the certificate and the Chief studied it before handing it back.

'Take a good look at the details on that certificate,' he invited. 'Tell me if they're all correct.'

Conway looked at him blankly for a moment and then obediently ran his eye over the document. 'Oh yes,' he said flatly, in the tone of one coming across some tiny forgotten particular. 'It says bachelor. I was actually a widower. My first wife had died some years before.'

'Was it you gave the details at the register office?' Kelsey asked.

Conway nodded. 'Anna and I went to the office together. We each gave our own details.'

'Why did you say you were a bachelor?'

'We'd better sit down,' Conway said with an air of patient resignation. 'I hadn't told Anna I'd been married before,' he began when they were all seated. 'When we first met it simply never arose. It wasn't something I felt like mentioning casually. It had taken me a long time to get over the death of my first wife to any extent at all.'

He gave the Chief a level look. 'I don't imagine I need go into the circumstances of Ida's death, I imagine you're well aware of them by now. I never talked about Ida to anyone, I did my best to put it all behind me.

'When I first mentioned marriage to Anna—when she was working at the Parkway Café—I fully intended, naturally, to tell her about my first marriage. But I had to pick my moment, I couldn't just blurt it out in a couple of sentences. I'd been very fond of Ida, her death was a terrible shock.' He drew a long breath. 'I could understand why Anna never wanted to talk about the past, I felt the same way myself over Ida.

'But then things broke up with Anna, before I'd got round to telling her. Later, when we met up again, she was in such a state over Reardon's death, I could hardly start telling her then about Ida, the way she'd died, it would have been a lunatic thing to do, Anna was in a bad enough way already. By the time we got around to discussing marriage again, Anna was a lot steadier. I did think seriously about telling her then. But when it came to it I couldn't take the risk of upsetting her again when she was so much calmer. I decided to let it go for the time being.'

He moved his shoulders. 'I honestly couldn't see it would be any great crime to put myself down as a bachelor. I was legally free to marry again. I intended to tell Anna as soon as the time seemed right. I was going to get the marriage certificate amended as soon as I'd told her.'

Kelsey regarded him in silence, then he asked: 'Who is the executor of Anna's will?'

'I am,' Conway responded.

'Was her will drawn up by a solicitor?'

Conway shook his head. 'She drew it up herself. It was very straightforward. We both made our wills at the same time. We bought the forms at a stationer's.'

'Do you have her will here?'

'Yes, I have.' He produced it from the bureau; a brief, simple document. Kelsey frowned down at it. 'I see everything is left "to David Malcolm Conway", not "to my husband, David Malcolm Conway". Why is that?'

Conway went to the bureau again and brought over his own will. 'You'll see this is expressed in the same way. Everything is left "to Anna Marie Conway", not "to my wife, Anna Marie Conway". I'd been along to the reference library to look up the point and I was as certain as I could be that the marriage wasn't invalidated because I'd put bachelor on the certificate instead of widower, but just in case there could possibly be any doubt or delay over that, I decided not to make any reference in my will to Anna being my wife. Then, if I died before I'd had a chance to tell Anna about my first marriage and get the certificate amended, she would be certain to get everything I left.

'I sat down and wrote my will first. Anna read it over and she asked me the same question: Why hadn't I put "to

my wife, Anna Marie Conway"? Of course I couldn't tell
her the real reason, so I just said it could be done either
way, I preferred that way. When she sat down to write her
own will a few minutes later, she simply copied what I'd
done.'

'You realize, of course, that the same thing holds good
for you,' Kelsey commented. 'If there should be any question
of the validity of the marriage, you will still inherit everything Anna left.'

By way of reply Conway made an abrupt gesture of
dismissal as if such a thought had never entered his head.

'When you left Bredon House,' Kelsey went on, 'to go to
work at Dorrell's store, and then again, later, when you left
Dorrell's and went to work at Ackroyd's, you gave yourself
out at both places as a single man.'

'That's not strictly correct,' Conway protested. 'Both
times, when I was being interviewed for the job, I was asked
if I was married. Both times I just said no. If any of them
had gone on to ask: Does that mean you're single, widowed
or divorced? I'd have told them I was a widower, of course
I would, no reason not to. But I wasn't asked and I didn't
volunteer the information. I can't see that it matters in the
slightest.'

'When you left Ackroyd's to go to Zodiac you didn't tell
the Ackroyds you were getting married.'

Conway smiled slightly. 'I take it you've met Mrs Ackroyd?'

Kelsey nodded.

'Then you'll appreciate my position, you know the kind
of woman she is. She'd never have rested till she'd met
Anna, grilled her, pumped her dry, ferreted out every last
little morsel about her past—and mine. It wouldn't be very
long before she'd got hold of the facts of Reardon's death.'
He gave a brief shudder. 'You can imagine the meal she'd
have made of all that.'

He gave the Chief a direct look. 'When I went after the
Zodiac job I made no secret there of the fact that I was

getting married, they knew that was one of the main reasons why I wanted a change.'

The Chief switched tack. 'When you first mentioned marriage to Anna, when she was working at the Parkway, you told her you were in no position to buy a house. What about the money you inherited from Ida Willett? Couldn't you have used that to buy a house?'

'It was nowhere near enough to buy any kind of house outright, let alone the sort of house Anna wanted,' Conway explained in a tone of resolute patience. 'Ida's flat was nothing luxurious, it was no great size. And there had been a terrific jump in property prices since I inherited the money.' He flung out a hand. 'If Anna's attitude had been different, I would have used the money as a deposit on a small house or flat, taken out a mortgage for the rest.'

He went back to his desk and put away the documents. He stood hesitating, then he stooped and pulled open a lower drawer. He lifted out a small wooden box, unlocked it with a key from his pocket. He took out a studio photograph and handed it to Kelsey. It showed a pretty girl with a happy smile, dark eyes, a wealth of dark hair.

'That's Ida.' Conway's voice held mingled affection and sorrow. 'Taken when she was eighteen, just before she married Willett. I never knew her like that, of course, young and happy, starting out in life, but it's how I like to think of her. That's the only photograph I kept of her. I had to keep it locked away as long as Anna didn't know about my first marriage.'

He went back to his desk and replaced the photograph in the wooden box. He was on the point of locking the box again when he checked himself. 'No need for that any more,' he said in a low voice. He put a hand up to his face. 'Force of habit.' He put the box away in the drawer, turned and glanced across at the Chief. 'Have you met Gregory Willett?'

The Chief nodded.

'Not a very savoury gentleman, in my book. I only ever met him once, on the day of the inquest on Ida. I knew all about his marriage to Ida, she'd told me the whole story.'

He remained leaning against the desk. 'She didn't know Willett long before they were married, he was only a clerk at the time. She thought they'd have an ordinary, pleasant life together but she soon found out he had very different ideas. He was going to get on and no one was going to stop him. She was afraid she wouldn't be able to keep up. He spent hardly any time at home, he always had something on the boil.

'She thought they'd have a family, she could devote herself to the children. But it was a few years before she had a child, a boy, and she was told then she'd never be able to have another. He was the apple of her eye, she built her whole life round him. She gave up all attempt to keep pace with her husband.

'When the boy was ten he went away to summer camp and picked up meningitis. He was dead in no time at all. She couldn't take it in, it was too sudden, too overwhelming. Willett's remedy was to throw himself even more into work.'

He began to pace the room. 'She started drinking, to help her get through the days. Willett found someone else, years younger than Ida, the daughter of a well-to-do local businessman. Ida got wind of what was going on, she drank more than ever. She lost all confidence, she had no social life, no friends left.

'One day Willett put a proposition to her. He wanted a divorce, but there must be no fuss, no scandal. If she would go along with that he would buy her a little flat, hand over a lump sum, pay her agreed alimony. But he wanted something more and he was willing to pay for it.

'He was well into local politics by then. He wanted her to move right away from the town, give her word never to go near the place again, never to contact him or his new wife—keep away and keep her mouth shut, is what it boiled down to. If she'd agree, he would be a lot more generous, he would pay her an additional allowance every month as well as the alimony, he'd go on paying the extra as long as she kept her side of the bargain.

'She accepted the offer, she couldn't see much alternative. She went to live in Graysholt, a town she'd never set foot in, where she didn't know a living soul. She went on drinking. She kept her bargain with Willett, she kept it to the end.'

He dropped into a chair. 'She'd been divorced three or four years when I met her.' He stared at the wall. 'On the day of the inquest Willett hung about the court house car park with his solicitor, to catch me before I went inside. He made out he wanted to offer me his sympathy but it was crystal clear what he was after—making sure I didn't have any nasty ideas about trying to make trouble for him over her death. It was a bitterly cold day but he was in a muck sweat, terrified it might come out how he'd treated Ida, it might get back to his precious voters.

'I was pretty well flaked out at the time, I'd been knocked sideways by her death. I was in no state to make trouble for anyone. Not that I wanted to. Ida was dead, nothing could bring her back or help her any more. I made it clear to Willett he'd nothing to fear from me.

'After the inquest he came over and spoke to me again. I could see he was cock-a-hoop at the verdict, the way everything had gone so smoothly for him, though he did his best to play it down.'

His face wore a look of revulsion. 'It stuck out a mile he was delighted Ida was dead, she could never embarrass him now. He didn't come to the funeral, didn't send any flowers. I never set eyes on him again.' His voice was fiercely contemptuous. 'Nor wanted to.'

CHAPTER 15

Sergeant Lambert walked up the steps of the police station next morning feeling a trifle the worse for wear. It had been turned nine-thirty last evening by the time he had ravenously attacked his dried-up supper. It had lain like lead on his stomach all night; he had slept wretchedly.

But if he was hoping for a relatively easy day he was doomed to disappointment.

'Biddulph,' the indefatigable Chief announced the instant their paths crossed. 'The family Conway worked for before he went to Bredon House.' A purposeful glint shone in his green eyes. 'Get hold of the address. We'll nip over there as soon as maybe.'

They managed to get away in the early afternoon. It seemed there was no longer anyone by the name of Biddulph living in the old family home—a small William and Mary manor house on the edge of a village some ten miles from Graysholt. The property had passed through more than one pair of hands in recent times and was now owned by a retired army colonel who financed his gentlemanly way of life by running the manor as an upmarket guesthouse during the holiday season.

It was an afternoon of brilliant autumn sunshine. Their route took them through well-kept countryside, its mellow tints of sepia, terracotta, olive, giving it the look of a landscape in an old Italian oil painting. They passed a hunt in full cry across the fields. Soon afterwards they came in sight of the manor.

The gates were closed but the house was clearly visible at the head of the drive. Built of brick with stone dressings; ornamental chimneys, tall windows, a broad flight of steps. It might be considered small as manor houses go but it would have made three or four of any normal-sized dwelling.

As they got out of the car Kelsey saw a tall, lean man in country tweeds and a deerstalker hat walking down the drive at a smart pace with a pair of English setters at his heels. He sent an inquiring look in their direction.

Kelsey went over to him as he let himself out through the wicket gate. He introduced himself and indicated his errand.

'I'm afraid I can't be of much help,' the colonel said in response to Kelsey's question about the Biddulph family. 'I never knew them. Before my time. But I do know who ought to be able to help you. Odd-job chappie in the village. He's worked at the manor on and off since he left school. He's doing a spot of decorating in the old schoolhouse, just now.' He gave them directions. 'Tell him I sent you.'

The odd-job chappie was hard at work painting exterior window-frames at the schoolhouse. He had no objection to breaking off, after a due word with the householder. He sat down with the two policemen on a garden bench.

He remembered old Mr Biddulph well. 'When I first started working at the manor,' he told them, 'he was hale and hearty, as normal as you or me. He wouldn't be much over sixty then, big, heavy-built chap. I did notice after a time his memory wasn't always so good. It got worse over the years. His wife had been dead a long time, they never had any children. He did have a niece, Miss Biddulph, she was the only relative he had left.

'She didn't live in these parts but she came over to see him two or three times a year. By the time he was knocking on for eighty you'd have to say he was getting senile, so Miss Biddulph came to live at the manor to look after him, generally take over the running of the place. She wouldn't be far off forty by that time. The old man died about two years after she moved in.' He shook his head. 'Terrible thing to happen, a nice old chap like that. Miss Biddulph was very upset about it.'

Kelsey asked him what had happened.

'I wasn't working at the manor at the time,' he pointed

out, 'so I only know what I read in the papers, and what
they said in the village.'

'And what was that?'

'Miss Biddulph had the builders in at the time, doing
some repairs to the property. Chimneystacks, roof, some of
the brickwork, wanted seeing to. They had quite a bit of
scaffolding up. Seems the old man got out of bed and went
wandering round the house. Ended up on the roof. Fell off
and broke his neck.'

'Did anyone hear anything in the night?'

'It seems not. Miss Biddulph had pensioned off the old
servants when she took over, she made do with daily women
from the village. There was just the one lad living in at the
time the old man died, and he didn't sleep in the house. He
had a little room over the old stables.'

'Do you know what his name was?'

'Yes, I do. Conway, David Conway. He came to the
manor straight from school, to give a hand generally. He
was pretty useful all round but he was an absolute wizard
with a car. I used to slip him a bob or two to look after my
old jalopy. She'd go like the clappers after he'd been at her.'

'Do you know what happened to Conway after the old
man died?'

'He left when the manor was sold. He told me he was
going to work at some big posh store in Graysholt. I've
never run across him since. Bit out of our league, the missus
and me, posh stores in Graysholt. We do our shopping in
the village, or Brailshead.' He gestured into the distance.
'Brailshead's the nearest town. Not very big, but it's got
everything we want.'

It was almost five when Lambert pulled up before Brailshead police station. The senior officer who had looked into
Biddulph's death had been transferred elsewhere but a
uniformed constable who had been on the case was present
in the station. He recalled the incident clearly.

'Spreadeagled on the ground, he was,' he told Kelsey.

'The milkman found him around six in the morning. At the back of the house, by the scaffolding. All he had on was a pair of pyjamas. His slippers had come off when he'd climbed out, they were lying on the floor by the window, in a room at the top of the house, at the back. The bottom sash was raised right up.

'He'd had the same doctor thirty years or more. Alzheimer's disease, the doctor said he had. But he was in pretty good shape otherwise, he could have lived a good few more years, the Biddulphs were a long-lived family. The doctor said he was certainly spry enough to be able to climb out on to the scaffolding.'

There had been no disturbance in the night, the niece had heard nothing. 'There was a lad sleeping over the stables, he didn't hear anything, either.'

There had been nothing to suggest suicide. 'Very straightforward, the inquest. Accidental death. No blame attaching to anyone. Sympathy expressed with the niece.'

'The property went to her?'

'That's right. The will had been made out years before, long before she ever went to live at the manor, when the old man was still as right as rain. She sold up and left these parts.'

'This lad sleeping over the stables, was he a local lad?'

'Near enough. He came from Eastmill.' A town twelve miles away. 'When I asked him for his home address he told me he didn't have any home, only the room over the stables. He'd been in care most of his schooldays.'

Thursday dawned dank and misty. During the morning Sergeant Lambert rang the Eastmill Social Services Department and was able to make an appointment for the afternoon.

At three o'clock the two policemen were shown into the office of the supervisor who had had oversight of the later placements of David Malcolm Conway. The female social worker who had known Conway more closely and for considerably longer had left the service some time ago for less stressful employment.

Kelsey inquired about the circumstances which had brought Conway into care.

'It was before my time here,' the supervisor told him. 'I can only give you the bare facts but the local police will be able to fill in the details for you. David came into care when he was a few months over the age of five. He stayed in care till he was sixteen. He came in when his parents were arrested after the death of a brother who was one year older than David.'

CHAPTER 16

Kelsey asked how David had settled down in care.

'Fairly well,' the supervisor said. 'He was quiet and well behaved, never any trouble. But there was only ever one foster parent he managed to make any sort of close relationship with, a man who'd worked on the railway. He and his wife fostered children for us for years, they were never able to have any family of their own. The husband was pensioned off early after an accident at work.

'David was with them for about a year, then the man's health broke down and the wife gave up fostering to look after him.'

David had been considered bright at school but lacking interest in academic work. 'What he wanted was to get out into the world and start earning money. He found the Biddulph job for himself. He was very keen to get it. I could see why it attracted him. It was far enough away to give him a feeling of making a fresh start. And there was accommodation provided, that was a big factor, I'm sure. He'd have a home, without the strain of having to try to fit into a family. It would be a halfway house where he could take a look round, decide what he wanted to do, where to go from there. He didn't keep in touch with us after he started work. He wasn't the type to keep running back for advice.'

Kelsey asked if Conway had had any particular friend during his years in care.

There was one boy, he was told, also in care, a lad by the name of Sholto, in the same class at school. He was currently working as a wages clerk in a large industrial town some distance away.

There was no longer anyone in the Eastmill police station who had been involved in the investigation into the death of David Conway's older brother but a retired policewoman who had worked on the case was still living in the town. Kelsey rang her flat and found her in; she would be happy to talk to them.

She gave them a welcoming smile as she opened the door to them a few minutes later. A trim, grey-haired woman. She had never married, had devoted all her energies to the force, filled her days now with voluntary work.

She took them into her well-regulated kitchen and made them strong tea and hearty sandwiches as they talked.

A quarter of a century had gone by since David's parents had stood trial but the case was still fresh in her memory. She had seen many horrific sights in her years in the force but none worse than the battered, emaciated body of the elder Conway boy.

He hadn't been on any register of children at risk, wasn't under the supervision of the Social Services. He was almost seven years old at the time of his death but he had never attended any school, wasn't on the books of any doctor. His wretched existence had been totally unsuspected by anyone in authority until an hour or two before his death.

Kelsey asked how this could have come about.

'The parents lived in an isolated cottage on the edge of Eastmill,' the policewoman told them. The younger boy, David, started school in the ordinary way when he was five.

He was apparently an only child, reasonably well fed and clothed, quiet and docile.

One Monday morning, a few months after David started school, the existence of the older brother came suddenly to light when an ambulance was called to the cottage. The mother had run half a mile to the nearest phone-box as soon as her husband had left for work. She was distraught, she said the child had been playing in a local quarry, had slipped and fallen among rocks and boulders.

'The boy was in a coma when he was admitted to hospital, he had been in a coma for over twenty-four hours. He died later that morning. He had appalling head injuries, he was little more than a bag of bones.' The policewoman's voice shook. 'You couldn't put a finger between the bruises on his body.'

The post-mortem revealed a number of fractures, some recent, many old. Death had been caused by a fractured— or, more accurately, shattered—skull, in all probability caused by the child being snatched up by the heels and smashed several times against a wall. The condition of the skin showed that he had long been a stranger to daylight.

It was plainly a long time since he had possessed the strength to stand on his feet, let alone play in a quarry the best part of a mile from the cottage.

The father kept his mouth implacably shut but the mother broke down and talked.

It seemed that before the marriage both parents had worked in a factory in another town. He had paid her persistent attention but she had no interest in him, she was going with another man who worked at the same factory. A week or two after she discovered that she was pregnant, while she and her boyfriend were still digesting the news, the boyfriend was killed in an accident at the works. She was a helpless, dependent type, she had no family to turn to, she was assailed by panic.

The rejected suitor, no friend of the dead man, lost no

time in renewing his attentions. She told him the situation. He offered to marry her right away. She accepted.

He was at that time living at home with his elderly father in a cottage in an isolated position on the outskirts of town; the cottage belonged to the old man. The bride moved into the cottage. In due course the boy was born, a normal, healthy child.

Things went along smoothly enough at first. A year or so after the birth of the first child, David was born. Then the old man died and the cottage passed to his son. He had always had a fierce temper and he had always indulged in bouts of weekend drinking but he had kept both temper and drinking within bounds as long as his father was alive. Now this restraint was removed.

He had only ever tolerated the existence of the first-born boy, no son of his; now the child became the focus of his drunken rages.

His wife never actually joined in the assaults but she took no active steps to prevent them. In some way she felt the child's existence a reproach to herself, the circumstances of his birth unfitting him for normal treatment and consideration. She was herself the illegitimate child of a casual field worker, ill-treated by her mother. She never attempted to take the children and leave her husband. She had no friends, no neighbours, no one to help or advise her.

The maltreatment of the boy grew steadily worse, became habitual, impossible to disguise. She no longer allowed him out of the house, she locked him into a closet when she went shopping.

The time drew near when the boy must attend school—a step that couldn't even be contemplated; dire consequences would be certain to flow from it. The father solved the problem by selling the cottage and moving to Eastmill, where no one knew them. He found another factory job, bought another cottage in a similarly isolated position. The child's life continued on the same hideous course till the final savage assault.

'Any idea where the father is now?' Kelsey asked.

'He had a rough time of it in gaol,' the policewoman told him. 'He was lucky to get out in one piece when he'd served his time. He went up north, where he wasn't known. He started drinking again right away. He was stabbed in a pub brawl a few weeks later, he died on the pavement.'

'And his wife?'

'She served a few months of her sentence. Then one night in her cell she tore some of her clothes into strips and hanged herself.'

On this melancholy autumn evening there were few people about the damp streets of the industrial town where Sholto, Conway's old schoolfriend, lived. The homeward rush was over, the evening bustle not yet begun.

Sholto rented a cheap basement room in a tall Edwardian house in a decaying neighbourhood. The tiny front garden held a few tattered clusters of Michaelmas daisies.

When the police car pulled up outside the house, Sholto was doubly occupied. Clad in singlet and shorts, he was swinging a pair of bar-bells while at the same time attempting to follow an Italian lesson from a cassette. Olympic athletes in striking poses contemplated his efforts from brightly-coloured posters on the walls.

In spite of years of sweating and exercising he was still skinny and undersized with no pretensions whatever to looks.

At the knock on his door he set down his bar-bells, silenced the Italian teacher, plucked his dressing-gown from a hook, shrugged it on and snatched open the door.

The Chief identified himself and asked if they might come in.

Sholto didn't inquire their errand but at once stood aside and waved them in. He offered refreshments with an air of eagerness the Chief often encountered in lonely folk grasping at any friendly straw.

The Chief settled for coffee and Sholto plugged in the

kettle. From a corner of the crowded—though orderly—
room he produced sturdy folding chairs for his visitors.

'I understand,' the Chief began, 'you were at one time
friendly with a David Conway who was employed by a Miss
Biddulph, near Brailshead, till the death of her uncle.'

Sholto was taking beakers from a cupboard. He halted
and swung round. 'I always wondered,' he said on a lively
note, 'if anyone would ever start asking questions about the
old man's death, but I never thought it would take eleven
years.'

He broke off and darted a look of anxiety at the Chief. 'You
surely don't think David had anything to do with the old
man's death? I can assure you he didn't.' He grimaced. 'But
he had a pretty good notion of what happened that night.'

'You knew Conway well?' Kelsey asked.

'I knew him at school. Sometimes we'd land up in the
same children's home for a few weeks, between fosterings.'

'You kept in touch with him after you both left school?'

'Not really. We didn't live very near each other after we
started working, I only saw him once in a way. I read in the
paper about old Biddulph's death and the inquest. The next
time I saw David—it turned out to be the last time I ever saw
him—he told me the manor had been sold. He'd gone into
digs in Graysholt, he'd started work at Bredon House.'

The kettle came to the boil and he made instant coffee
and handed round the beakers. He took his own seat on the
edge of a table neatly stacked with books.

'What did David tell you about the old man's death?'
Kelsey wanted to know.

'He said things hadn't happened the way the police
believed. The night the old man died, David woke up with
one of his nightmares—he had nightmares all the time I
knew him, when we were at school. Lots of kids in care get
nightmares, I've certainly had my share of them. David's
used to be pretty bad. At one time he'd have them three or
four times a week but they gradually got better, till it was
only two or three times a month.

'He'd wake up terrified, sweating, his heart thumping so he thought he'd die. He used to jump out of bed and stick his head out of the window—he never slept with the window closed, just in case. He'd take deep breaths and after a few minutes it would slacken off and he'd get back into bed.

'The night the old man died, when David stuck his head out, he realized something was going on. There were lights on in the manor, folk moving about, he could hear noises. But he only half took it in, it was mixed up with his dream, he was trying to fight off the nightmare. He got back into bed and fell asleep.

'He was woken in the morning by all the commotion over finding the body. He had a word with Miss Biddulph before the police arrived, he told her what he'd seen and heard in the night. She was very pleasant, very kind. She told him he must have imagined it, it was part of his nightmare. It wouldn't be a good idea to say anything to the police about it, it would only confuse matters.

'So he kept his mouth shut. Miss Biddulph never mentioned it again. She was very helpful to him over the Bredon House job, she pulled a string or two for him with the store, gave him a wonderful testimonial. And when she sold the manor she handed him a cheque for five thousand pounds. She said part of it was by way of a redundancy payment and the rest was a bonus as he'd been such a loyal employee. He was bowled over, he hadn't expected anything. It was a tremendous sum to him.'

'I understand Miss Biddulph left the district?' Kelsey said.

'That's right. She went to Spain, David said. I imagine her boyfriend went with her.'

'Boyfriend?' Kelsey echoed.

'Yes, she had a boyfriend, from before she went to live at the manor. He used to go over to the manor in the evenings, always after the staff had gone home. David was certain he was one of the two people he'd seen moving about, the night the old man died—the other person was

Miss Biddulph. He'd said so to her when he spoke to her about what he'd seen. She was very anxious he shouldn't mention the boyfriend to the police. She said there was no reason for them even to know of his existence, it would only involve him in something that was nothing to do with him, it would be a waste of police time. So David said nothing.'

Sholto drank his coffee. 'It would be great to see David again, but he made it pretty plain that last time that he wanted to cut right away from the past, make a new life. I could understand that very well.' He made a wry face. 'I've done my best over the years to forget my own past. I'm sure David will have done all right for himself, he was a lot cleverer than me at school, and he was always keen to get somewhere in life.'

He tilted back his head. 'I used to think he'd try for a job with cars, or trains. He was mad about trains. One place where he was fostered, the man used to take him train-spotting. Sometimes he'd get him in to have a look round the engine sheds, he'd worked on the railway. Another place where he was fostered, the man used to deal in second-hand cars, doing them up and selling them. David got very interested in that, he used to hang around, helping him.'

His reminiscent smile revealed irregular teeth scrubbed snowy white, a surviving milk tooth. 'David was very good to me at school. I don't forget that. Before he came I was bullied a lot. I used to creep round everywhere, terrified out of my wits. He took me under his wing and looked after me. He was the best friend I ever had.'

CHAPTER 17

The funeral of Anna Marie Conway aroused no greater interest than her death or the inquest proceedings. The ceremony took place on Friday, at a crematorium some distance from Cannonbridge; a raw, showery morning when most folk preferred to stay indoors.

The clergyman, accustomed to conducting such services where, more often than not, he had never previously laid eyes on a single face in the congregation before him, strove to inject into the ritual procedure some sense of reverence, of sorrow for the untimely passing of a human life.

Neither of Anna's parents was present, nor, as far as Sergeant Lambert could ascertain, had either sent flowers. One blood relative had steeled herself to attend: Anna's maternal grandmother, Mrs Jefford. She drove over from Harvington alone, sat alone in the chapel, her back ramrod straight, elegant in her beautifully cut black suit. As the coffin began its farewell glide she wept silently, with digni-fied restraint.

Throughout, David Conway kept his eyes lowered. His pale face betrayed no emotion but as the congregation rose to leave the chapel Lambert observed his fists tight clenched at his sides.

They came out again into the chill morning. A skittering wind blew across from a nearby stretch of waste land. Mrs Jefford said a few words to the clergyman and then sought out Conway. Kelsey stood watching as she spoke to him, her face full of sympathy and concern.

The Chief turned his head and saw the Garbutts standing in the chapel porch, looking out at the bleak day. Irene had clearly been crying. Bob said something to her and her tears began to flow again. She plunged out of the porch and darted away on her own.

The Chief glanced back and saw Conway and Mrs Jefford shaking hands, then Conway went off towards the row of parked cars. Mrs Jefford came over to where Kelsey and Lambert stood in the shelter of the chapel wall. All three of them watched as Conway's car pulled out and drove away.

'Poor young man.' Mrs Jefford sighed deeply. 'He's devas-tated by it. At least Anna had some love in her life, that's something to remember.' She appeared in command of herself again. She was driving straight back to Harvington, to the demands of her busy life. She would attend the resumed inquest.

When she had gone Bob Garbutt walked across to speak to the Chief. 'Irene's taken it very much to heart,' he said with a shake of his head. He glanced over at his wife who was roaming the grounds, dabbing at her cheeks with a handkerchief, struggling for composure. 'She will have it she should have realized what state Anna was in, she shouldn't have been so busy with her own concerns. I keep telling her she's no call to go blaming herself, she couldn't be expected to be a mind-reader. If Anna chose to put a brave face on things, Irene couldn't be expected to see what she was really feeling underneath.'

He looked back at that Monday morning. 'Anna seemed happy enough to me, smiling and chatting. There was always something appealing about her, she always looked even younger than she was. I can see her now, standing there in her blue dressing-gown, with the porch light shining down on her.' He smiled slightly. 'She took out a handkerchief and wiped her mouth, like a kid that's been at the chocolate.'

Kelsey's head jerked round. 'At the chocolate?'

Garbutt raised a hand and described a circle round his lips. 'She had a bit of a stain round her mouth, like a kid that's been eating chocolate biscuits.'

Kelsey regarded him. 'It could have been the porch light casting shadows,' he suggested.

Garbutt shook his head with conviction. 'It was no shadow. I was right up by her, in the car. The driver's seat was next to the house, I could see her quite clearly. She looked down at her handkerchief, then she pulled a face and wiped her mouth again, more carefully. She was a very particular young woman, she was always very neat and clean.'

*

Inside five minutes they were back in the car again, headed
for Ferndale. 'Conway may not be there,' Lambert pointed
out. 'He may have gone straight off to work.'

Kelsey made no reply.

'Bob Garbutt never said anything before about seeing
Anna wipe her mouth that morning,' Lambert went on.
'A man like Garbutt, an ex-soldier, always driving round
Cannonbridge in his taxi, forever chatting to someone or
other, he's sure to be pally with some of the lads in the force.
He might very well know someone working at the mortuary.
Easiest thing in the world for him to pick up a few snippets
about the post-mortem.

'He hears about the chocolate in Anna's stomach, he
starts thinking back, he conjures up his last sight of her.
Doesn't take him long to convince himself he saw her
standing there with chocolate round her mouth. Next thing,
he's embroidering it a bit, he remembers her taking out her
handkerchief and wiping her lips. The more you query it,
the more certain he gets. Men like Garbutt like to see
themselves as keen-eyed and observant, never missing a
trick.'

Conway's beige-coloured Zephyr was standing in the drive-
way. As Lambert turned in through the gate the front door
of the bungalow opened and Conway came out, carrying a
briefcase. His head was lowered, his face set in thought.

He became aware of the police car. He stood motionless,
expressionless, as it came to a halt, then he walked across
to them.

'I was just leaving,' he said on a note of protest. 'I've got
appointments.'

'We won't keep you many minutes,' the Chief promised.
'We just want a word.'

Conway turned and led the way indoors. Everywhere
looked clean and orderly. In the sitting-room he sat them
down and took his own seat nearby on an upright chair. He
leaned forward with an air of concentrated attention, like a

man who intends to deal with the matter in hand with the utmost dispatch.

The Chief took him back to the statement he had made concerning the events of that Monday morning.

'You told us Anna had nothing of any kind to eat or drink before you left the house,' he began.

'That's perfectly correct,' Conway responded at once. 'That's how it always was.'

'Mr Garbutt told us just now that when Anna stood talking to him in the porch she had a mark round her mouth like a stain from chocolate. She took out a handkerchief and wiped her lips.'

Conway moved his head. 'I certainly never noticed anything like that. But if Bob says that's what he saw, then that's what he saw, he's not a man to dream things up. Anna was very fond of chocolate, she always had some by her.' He frowned in thought. 'She kept some in a jar in the bedroom. I suppose she could have eaten some of that without me knowing, while she was getting out of bed, putting on her dressing-gown.'

'Have you still got the dressing-gown?'

Conway nodded. 'I've still got all her things. I know I'll have to do something about them but I haven't been able—' He broke off. 'The dressing-gown's in the bedroom.'

'May we see it?'

'Yes, of course.'

On the way to the bedroom the Chief glanced along the passage and saw that the damaged bathroom door had been replaced by a brand-new one. Conway observed his look. 'I had that done a few days ago,' he said. 'They told me they could repair the old door but I couldn't have that. I wanted it out of the house. I couldn't bear the sight of it.'

In the bedroom he opened a cupboard and produced the blue dressing-gown, neatly folded. In the right-hand pocket Kelsey came upon a white handkerchief, a little crumpled but still bearing the sharp creases of diligent ironing—and some slight, brownish staining. He raised the handkerchief to his nose and sniffed, half persuading himself he could detect a lingering odour of chocolate.

Conway crossed to the cabinet on the left of the bed and took out the fancy glass jar Lambert had seen on their earlier visit. Conway handed the jar to the Chief and Kelsey removed the lid. Among the items of confectionery inside were some small, untouched bars of various kinds of chocolate—and part of a larger bar of milk chocolate, carefully folded back into its wrapper.

'Anna always kept chocolate biscuits in the kitchen, as well,' Conway recalled. He took them along and lifted a tin down from a shelf. Inside were two opened packets of biscuits: chocolate digestives and chocolate bourbons.

Kelsey shook his head. The contents of the stomach ruled out any such biscuits.

But they certainly didn't rule out the partly-eaten bar of milk chocolate in the bedroom.

CHAPTER 18

Chief Inspector Kelsey spent what was left of Friday clearing his desk. He was due to leave on Saturday morning for a conference the best part of a hundred miles away. He wouldn't get back to Cannonbridge till Monday evening.

The conference had been arranged months ago. He had not only agreed to attend, he had also blithely accepted an invitation to give a paper. In that rose-coloured moment the conference had seemed light-years away, he had all the time in the world to marshal his material, knock it into shape, revise and polish. Now the hour was upon him and he had yet to clarify a single thought, set down one solitary word.

When he got home to his flat on Friday evening he snatched a bite to eat before settling down to work on his paper. At midnight he called it a day, took a couple of aspirins to dispel the headache that had crept up on him and went to bed.

He slept heavily and woke at six. The headache, far from being dispelled, was now at full throttle. He knew with sickening finality the moment he crawled out of bed that his paper wouldn't do. He swallowed more aspirin, dispatched a sketchy breakfast and buckled down to work again.

At nine o'clock he was forced to abandon it. For good or ill, this was the paper he must now deliver. He had to bathe, shave, dress, throw a few things into a bag and get on his way. He cast a despairing glance at the clutter he was leaving behind. No time to tidy up. The sink was full of dirty crockery.

He had a sudden brief vision of his long-ago wife in the days—dreamlike now, largely forgotten—before their divorce. She had been a houseproud woman. She would have wrinkled her finely chiselled nose at the chaos reigning around him.

He blinked away her reproving image and scribbled a note to his cleaning woman who came in three times a week and was due again on Monday morning. He apologized for the mess, explained that he was going off for the weekend. Perhaps she could stay a little longer on Monday, give the place a good going-over? He would be very grateful.

In the event his conference paper was warmly applauded and provoked a good deal of lively discussion. He enjoyed the weekend, found it stimulating, if tiring. He stayed up far too late, talked too much, ate and drank more than was good for him.

Early on Monday evening he set off on the road home. As he drove, images of the conference gradually receded, thoughts of Ferndale and David Conway began to push up again into his mind.

He reached his flat soon after nine, ready for an early night. He let himself in, totally unprepared for the sight that greeted him: the flat in precisely the same state as he had left it, his note to the cleaning woman still propped up against the teapot. A deep groan escaped his lips.

Among the letters on the mat in the hall was a hand-delivered missive, dated Sunday, from the schoolboy son of his cleaning woman: his mother had gone down with 'flu, she wouldn't be back for a week or ten days.

Kelsey stood gazing about him disconsolately. Nothing for it but to roll up his sleeves and get stuck in; the thought of coming in from work tomorrow evening to face this lot was more than he could stomach.

He fortified himself with a pot of strong tea and set grimly about his chores. As he stood at the sink, pushed the vacuum cleaner over the carpet, wielded a mop or duster, his thoughts began to range again over the death of Anna Conway.

He was in bed soon after eleven and slept soundly all night. He bounded up the station steps next morning, brimful of energy.

Sergeant Lambert was waiting for him with a couple of queries that had arisen while he was away, but the Chief waved a dismissive hand. 'Later.' His green eyes bored into Lambert. 'You remember Conway gave us the names of two passengers he said travelled with him on the train that morning.' A lad by the name of Colin Opie, working on a farm under a youth training scheme. And a middle-aged conveyancing clerk called Mottram. 'We'll have a word with those two. Today, if possible.'

He surveyed his desk, bearing abundant evidence of his absence. 'Doubt if we'll make it before this afternoon.'

The day proved even busier than the Chief had foreseen and it was close on six when they finally managed to get away.

The farm where Colin Opie worked lay a quarter of a mile from one of the stations on the steam line. Darkness had descended over the fields as Lambert drove up to the farmhouse.

The Chief asked if he might speak to Colin. The farmer offered no objection once he was satisfied the lad wasn't in any kind of trouble. He pointed out a brightly-lit, open-fronted shed where Colin was busy cleaning a tractor. Rain began to spatter down as they crossed the yard.

Colin turned out to be a fresh-faced lad with a cheerful look, an open manner. He was pleased to be able to help in any way he could after the Chief had trotted out one of his vague spiels to explain why the police should suddenly display curiosity about a train ride two weeks earlier.

Colin told them he lived in at the farm during the week, going back home—a village five stations along the steam line—every Saturday afternoon and returning on Monday morning.

He was a steam enthusiast, working when he could over the weekend at his local station back home. In the course of his travels on the line he had struck up an acquaintance with Conway. But he knew nothing of Conway's personal circumstances; he didn't know precisely where he lived, or if he was married. Conway's manner never invited personal questions, even if Colin had been minded to ask them—which he wasn't.

Colin boarded the train three stops before Oldmoor, where Conway got on. Colin got off again two stops past Oldmoor, leaving Conway to continue to Sedgefield Junction, where a main-line train would carry him on to Dunstall.

The Chief asked if Colin could be more precise about the train timings.

'I've got all the different steam-line leaflets in my room,' Colin declared with pride. 'They'll tell you anything you need to know: maps, schedules, times, links with the main line. You can take any you want to, if you'd like to come up to the house. I can easily pick up some more for myself.'

Kelsey asked what Colin could recall about Conway's manner that Monday morning. Had he behaved in any way differently from usual?

'I remember he was very quiet that morning.' Colin grinned. 'It seemed to be me doing all the talking. Usually he was very interested in everything that was going on. He'd be looking out of the window, telling me about famous locomotives he'd seen, engine sheds he'd been into when he was a lad. But that morning, one or two remarks I made, he didn't answer, he seemed to be miles away. I asked him if he had a headache.'

He grinned again. 'I had to ask him twice before it got through to him. That sort of woke him up. He said he was fine and after that he did try to pay more attention. I thought he probably had some business problem bothering him.'

It was raining heavily by the time they reached Mottram's residence in a quiet suburb of a small town lying between Sedgefield Junction and Dunstall.

An enticing aroma of cooking greeted them as Mrs Mottram opened the door. A pleasant-looking woman with a friendly smile. Yes, they could speak to her husband. He hadn't been in long, he was occupying the time before supper wrestling with the children's homework.

She showed the two policemen into a sitting-room and went to summon her husband. He came along a minute or two later. Tall and lean, with a courteous, affable manner.

Once again Kelsey had to recite one of his reassuring spiels. Mottram didn't swallow it anywhere near as easily as Colin Opie had done but he refrained from pursuing the matter and cooperated readily enough.

He told them he travelled daily to his work in Dunstall by main-line train. He got on the train at the station after Sedgefield Junction. On Conway's occasional trips to the Dunstall factory he made a point of looking out of the window for Mottram as he boarded the train; they had started chatting during the journey a few months ago.

He knew nothing of Conway personally. They usually chatted about business, politics and so on. And Mottram was always interested to hear anything Conway had to tell him about the steam railway. He had been an enthusiast in his younger days and still took his family for Sunday trips on the steam railway during the summer.

On that Monday morning he and Conway had left the train as usual at Dunstall. They had walked together out on to the forecourt where a colleague of Conway's was parked, waiting to give Conway his customary lift to the factory, five minutes' drive away, in the opposite direction from Mottram's office.

Mottram had some slight acquaintance with this colleague of Conway's; he had handled the conveyance of a property for him twelve months ago, when the colleague had sold his flat and bought a house. Mottram put his head in at the car window and chatted with the colleague for a minute or two—a little light-hearted badinage about the jollifications due to follow the Zodiac sales meeting. The car then drove off with Conway inside and Mottram went off on the short walk to his office.

The Chief asked if Conway had behaved as usual that morning.

Mottram pondered. 'He seemed in very good spirits. He was lively, talked a lot. I guessed he was probably looking forward to the celebrations at Zodiac.'

He smiled as a thought struck him. 'I shall pull his leg next time I see him. I asked him if he'd had a good trip on the steam train, if it was spot on time, and so on. He told me yes, it had been a very smooth run, very punctual.' He laughed. 'And the fact of the matter was, the train was actually ten minutes late that morning getting into Sedgefield Junction!'

'Ten minutes late?' Kelsey echoed.

'That's right,' Mottram declared with amusement. 'It was held up, half way along the loop line. I happened to hear about it on the local radio that evening. For all Conway makes out he's such an enthusiast, I reckon he must have dozed off, missed what was happening.'

He laughed again. 'Even so, you'd think he couldn't help noticing his train was late at the junction. He must have had to pick up his feet and run like blazes to get over to the main-line platform in time to catch the train for Dunstall.'

CHAPTER 19

The rain was bucketing down as they came out of Mottram's house and ran back to the car. The Chief switched on the interior light and took out the railway brochures Colin Opie had given him. Beautifully produced in colour on glossy paper, every detail meticulously set out, the precise distance between stops, the exact time every train might be expected to enter and leave every station.

'Conway didn't know the steam train had broken down,' Kelsey said grimly, 'because he wasn't on the train when it broke down. He got off very soon after Colin Opie left. He went back to Ferndale and disposed of Anna. Then he went off to Sedgefield Junction and got on the Dunstall train, sat himself down, all innocent and serene, ready to stick his head out of the window at the next stop, looking for Mottram.'

He studied a map of the steam route. The next stop after Opie got off was Blakestone, a small country station. Immediately after Blakestone the steam line swung off in a long loop to service outlying hamlets, curling up again to its terminus at Sedgefield Junction.

'That's where Conway got off: Blakestone.' Kelsey jabbed at the map. 'It would give him the maximum time for what he had to do. And he'd need every minute he could get. He'd have to drive back to Ferndale pretty smartish. He would already have given Anna the hot chocolate when he woke her up.'

Rain hammered on the roof of the car. 'It's my belief,' Kelsey declared, 'that Conway had made a habit for some time—ever since he worked out the details of his plan—of going into the bedroom to say goodbye to Anna before he left for work in the morning, however early it was, taking her in the hot chocolate, strong and sweet.' Conway would have gone to some trouble to establish the custom, probably made a charming little ritual of it, got her well and truly used to it, so there'd be no question but that she'd drink her hot chocolate down that Monday morning. Only this time the chocolate would be laced with pills, and he'd have made it even stronger and sweeter than usual, to cover up the taste.

'By the time he got back to the bungalow,' Kelsey went on, 'she'd be in a drowsy, couldn't-care-less state. She'd have very little idea of what was happening to her, she certainly wouldn't be able to put up any resistance.' Conway would deal with her soothingly and disarmingly until the very last moment, when she lay back in the rose-scented water, on the verge of sleep, and he took out the pocket-knife.

'Then off again to Sedgefield Junction, as fast as maybe, to catch the train for Dunstall.' Kelsey studied the times listed. The steam train took a leisurely fifty minutes to traverse the loop but the distance across the top of the loop, as a car would travel, was no more than a mile or two.

There was a wait of fourteen minutes between the arrival of the steam train at Sedgefield Junction and the departure of the main-line train for Dunstall. That would give Conway just over an hour between stepping off the steam train at Blakestone and boarding the main-line train for Dunstall at Sedgefield Junction.

'I reckon he could do it,' the Chief declared.

Sergeant Lambert was far from convinced. 'How is Conway supposed to be covering all this ground?' he asked on a strongly sceptical note. 'How is he getting from Blakestone to Ferndale, from Ferndale to Sedgefield Junction? What vehicle is he using? Garbutt drove him to Oldmoor station that morning, picked him up again at Oldmoor station on Monday evening. Conway's own car was in the garage at Ferndale on Monday night. I saw it there with my own eyes when we were leaving.' He had come out of the front door of the bungalow, just ahead of Conway, had walked across to the police cars. He had looked round for Conway, had spotted him a few yards away, opening the garage doors. He had walked over to tell Conway he needn't bother taking his own car, he could ride with them. Lambert had glanced inside the garage, had plainly seen Conway's beige Zephyr.

Kelsey moved his shoulders impatiently. 'Then he must have had a second car stashed away at Blakestone, close to the station, tuned up to tip-top form so he could rely on it not to let him down. He left the second car on the forecourt at Sedgefield Junction when he got on the train for Dunstall. He's had a good two weeks since then to go back to the junction and get rid of the car.'

He massaged his jaw. 'It'd have to be a car, too many snags with any other form of transport. And he'd need somewhere to keep the car, where he could work on it, tune it up, away from his wife's eye—and from Garbutt's eye, for that matter.' He stared out at the water cascading down the windscreen. 'It must have been that way. It's the only way he could have done it.'

'If he did it.' Lambert's tone hadn't shifted from deep scepticism.

'He did it all right,' Kelsey declared with certainty. He suddenly struck his hands together. 'That's why he ordered the box of fruit from Garbutt for that Monday morning! So Anna would get up and go along to speak to Garbutt. Conway had to have a witness to prove beyond all doubt that Anna was alive and well when he left the house. Garbutt was the only possible witness.'

He sat frowning out at the relentless rain. 'What we need now is a detailed map of the area round Blakestone station.' Showing every last property, every garage, every shed capable of housing a car. Too late to do anything about it this evening; they'd get cracking on it first thing in the morning.

*

By mid-afternoon on Wednesday Kelsey had his map spread
out on his desk, together with a note of the occupants of
every dwelling. He sat with Lambert beside him, knitting
his brows in concentration.

'It's got to be one of those three houses.' Kelsey stabbed
a finger at the map. The houses stood at some distance from
each other, at different points of the compass. He consulted
the list of occupants. The first house could be struck off at
once: a married couple with small children, a family car.
The second house was no better: man, wife, grown-up
daughter, all three of them with cars.

He considered the third house, standing in a secluded
spot behind a belt of tall trees. Large garden, garage well
away from the house, out of sight and earshot of it, in no
way overlooked by any other dwelling; the garage gave on
to a quiet lane. The sole occupant of the property was an
elderly widow, a Mrs Egan. She hadn't owned a car for
several years.

'That's the one!' the Chief declared with total conviction.
'Or I'm a Dutchman.'

In the comfortable sitting-room of her villa behind its screen
of trees, Mrs Egan was engaged in one of her less favourite
occupations: dusting her crowded bookshelves. From the
cushioned ease of an armchair by the fire a Burmese cat,
old enough now to be sedate, lazily watched her. The radio
spun a cheerful web of music.

As Mrs Egan stepped on to a footstool to reach a
higher shelf she heard the doorbell ring. 'Whoever can
that be?' she demanded of the cat. It offered no reply.
She stepped down again, very carefully on account of her
treacherous back and uncertain knees. She glanced about
for her stick. She went slowly and stiffly from the room
and along the passage.

On the doorstep, Sergeant Lambert pressed the bell a
second time, more loudly. He had pulled up by the garage
a few minutes before, to allow the Chief to survey the

terrain and peer in through the garage windows. The garage stood empty.

They heard the sound of slow movement inside the house. The front door opened and a frail-looking old woman gazed questioningly out at them.

'Mrs Egan?' Kelsey inquired. She gave a nod. He explained who he was, told her he would like to ask her a few questions about her garage.

'You'd better come inside,' she said at once. She looked enlivened at the prospect of diversion. She led the way, step by cautious step, back to the sitting-room.

'You'll have some tea?' she invited, but Kelsey declined politely, envisaging the protracted performance that was likely to prove.

She switched off the radio and ousted the cat from its chair. When they were all three seated to her satisfaction she looked expectantly across at the Chief. 'Well, now, what is it you would like to know?'

He asked if she had let her garage to anyone in recent months.

Yes, as it happened, she had. She had let it in the third week of September. 'To a business gentleman,' she told him. 'He took it till the end of October. He offered me a very good rent and he paid the whole lot there and then, in cash.' She smiled in reminiscent pleasure. 'He was no trouble at all. I never set eyes on him again. At the end of October, when the let was up, I found the key slipped through my letter-box.'

Kelsey asked if she knew the name of this business gentleman.

She looked regretful. 'I'm afraid not. He did tell me but I can't remember. And he told me what firm he worked for, but I can't remember that, either—I had no reason to remember. He did give me one of his business cards but I've no idea what I did with it.' She glanced vaguely about. 'I expect it got thrown away.'

She looked earnestly across at the Chief. 'I don't know

why you're interested in him, and it's not my place to ask, but he didn't look to me at all the sort of man I'd ever expect the police to come asking about. He was very pleasant, nicely spoken, he seemed very respectable.' She smiled. 'He wore a very good suit, and his shoes were beautifully polished.'

No, she had never laid eyes on whatever car he had kept in the garage. 'It's a long time since I managed to get down to that part of the garden,' she admitted wryly.

Kelsey produced Conway's photograph and she stared fixedly down at it. 'I really couldn't say if that's the man,' she said at last. 'I only ever saw him the once.' She cocked her head to one side. 'I suppose it could be him, but if you showed me a dozen different photos, I dare say I'd say the same about half of them.' She hesitated, then she ventured: 'I suppose he must have been mixed up in something or you wouldn't be here, asking questions.'

'That doesn't necessarily follow,' Kelsey told her. 'It's just a routine inquiry. And we may not even be talking about the same man.'

She looked greatly relieved. 'I'm very glad to hear you say that. I was beginning to think Mr Yealland was right after all.'

'Mr Yealland?' Kelsey queried.

'He and his wife do a few hours' work for me every week. He worked on a local farm till he retired. They're very good, very reliable, I don't know how I'd manage here without them. She does a bit of cleaning and shopping. He keeps the garden tidy and does odd jobs about the place.

'I mentioned to him that I'd let the garage.' She made a little face. 'He was distinctly disapproving. I believe he thought I ought to have consulted him before I let the garage to a total stranger. He does go on a bit sometimes. Once he gets something between his teeth he does tend to hang on to it. But one can't be cross with him, his heart's in the right place. And he does watch out for my interests, makes sure nobody tries to diddle me.'

She smiled. 'He asked me how much rent I'd been paid

for the garage.' A triumphant gleam shone from her eye. 'When he heard how much it was, he had to admit I'd done a very good stroke of business.'

Before they left, the Chief asked her for Yealland's address. She directed them to a cottage standing on its own down a lane a few minutes' drive away.

But the cottage was in darkness when they drove up; no one at home. The Chief looked at his watch. Six-fifteen. 'We'll get on over to Ferndale,' he instructed Lambert. 'Conway should be home by now.'

On the Chief's direction Sergeant Lambert didn't approach Ferndale by the usual route but took a side road, pulling up in a sheltered spot under the drooping branches of a clump of trees alongside the rear garden of the bungalow.

The Chief got out of the car. A few paces took him to a gate giving entry to the garden. The back door of the dwelling faced him a short distance away.

He got back into the car and told Lambert to start up again, drive round and in through the front gate, as usual.

Conway's car wasn't in evidence but light showed from the sitting-room. Conway answered the door without delay, still wearing his business suit. He looked in better spirits, less pale and strained. He showed no surprise or irritation, didn't ask why they'd called. He greeted them pleasantly and invited them in.

They followed him into the sitting-room where he had been working at his desk. He offered refreshments but the Chief didn't accept.

Kelsey lost no time in getting down to brass tacks. He asked Conway to cast his mind back to that Monday morning, outline again briefly how he had spent the time between leaving Ferndale and eleven o'clock that morning—by eleven, at the latest, according to the pathologist, Anna Conway was well and truly dead.

Conway raised no objection. He had left the house at seven-fifteen with Bob Garbutt. Garbutt had driven him to

Oldmoor station. He had joined Colin Opie on the steam train at around seven-thirty, had chatted to Opie, who left the train two stops later. He had remained on the train round the loop line, getting off at the terminus, Sedgefield Junction.

At this point Kelsey broke into his account to ask if the journey on the steam train had been as usual that morning.

'There was a delay at one point,' Conway told him. 'The train was held up for ten minutes half way along the loop.'

'How did the passengers react to that?'

Conway smiled. 'It caused quite a stir.'

'And yet, when Mottram asked you what kind of trip you'd had, you never mentioned the delay.'

'Didn't I?' Conway moved his shoulders. 'I dare say I had other things on my mind.' He smiled again. 'All the hoo-ha ahead of me at Zodiac that day, for one thing.'

At Sedgefield Junction he had gone across to the main line to board the 8.50 for Dunstall. He had to hurry because of the delay on the steam line. The 8.50 had left on time, he had caught it with only a few seconds to spare.

He looked out for Mottram at the next stop, chatted to him as usual. They left the train together at Dunstall where a colleague was waiting to give him a lift to the works. Mottram spoke briefly to his colleague and then went off to his own office.

At the works he and his colleague went together to the stockrooms to look over the latest deliveries of job lots and chance-bought materials. They had remained together all the time they were in the stockrooms. They then went along to the sales meeting together. The meeting started punctually at nine forty-five and finished a minute or two before eleven. He had sat beside this colleague throughout the meeting.

The Chief asked for the colleague's name and address and Conway supplied them.

Had Conway left the sales meeting at any point?

Conway shook his head with a look of some amusement.

'I certainly did not. No one leaves a Zodiac sales meeting before it finishes, I can assure you of that.'

'When did you first start travelling to Dunstall by train instead of driving over there in your car?' Kelsey wanted to know.

'The first time was in April. My first sales meeting was in March, not long after I'd joined the firm, I drove over for it in my car. When I heard about the steam railway I went along to Oldmoor station and got hold of timetables— I've always been interested in steam.

'I realized I could make the journey to Dunstall that way. I didn't need my car in Dunstall, I was always at the factory, and I could easily get a lift to and from the station. Zodiac accounts told me they'd pay the normal car mileage for the journey and I could stand the extra myself. It was only once every four weeks so I decided I'd treat myself.'

'When did you start using Garbutt's taxi to take you to and from Oldmoor station for your trip to the factory?'

'Right from the first time I went by train, in April.'

'Why did you use the taxi? Why not drive to the station in your own car, leave it at the station, pick it up again when you got back? It would have saved you a bob or two.'

Conway reacted with energy. 'Maybe so, but it would have meant taking a risk with my car.' He made a sharply dismissive gesture. 'I'd never dream of leaving a car of mine on a stretch of waste ground at the mercy of any passing yobbo—there's no proper car park at the station, no supervision. I'd get back as likely as not to find the paintwork scratched, wing mirrors bent. I might even find the car stolen—that would be a big help in my job. No, thank you very much, that's not my idea of things. My car belongs to me, not to the firm. I take very good care of any car I own.'

'And how many cars do you own?'

'One,' Conway answered promptly.

'Have you owned a second car in recent times?'

'Yes, I have.' Again no hesitation.

'How did you come to own a second car?'

Conway's face exhibited signs of distress. He bent his head. His voice was low and unsteady.

'I bought a little second-hand car towards the end of September. It was going to be a birthday present for Anna— her birthday's October 30th. I bought it early so I could work on it. I wanted to get it into first-class condition.'

He raised his head, his voice grew stronger. 'I always do the work on any car I own. I know too much about garages and what they get up to, I wouldn't trust one of them to work on a car of mine. I knew a man years ago who dealt in cars, I saw some of the tricks of the trade then. Enough to make your hair stand on end.

'I was going to start teaching Anna to drive after she got back from her holiday. I thought she'd be up to it by then. It was Dr Peake suggested teaching her to drive, getting her a little car. He thought it would encourage her to get out and make friends, take up new interests, give her confidence.'

'Where did you keep this car?'

'I rented a garage in Blakestone.'

'Why Blakestone?'

Conway shrugged. 'I'd no particular reason for choosing Blakestone. It was just where I happened to find a garage.'

'Surely you could have found a garage nearer than that?'

'I didn't know any house round here with an empty garage. And I wouldn't have wanted it too near Ferndale in case Anna got to hear about it.' His voice trembled again. 'I particularly wanted it to be a surprise. It would have been her first birthday that we'd spent together as husband and wife. She'd have been twenty. That seemed a landmark, the end of her teens.'

He looked across at Kelsey. 'I knew from little things she'd said that she'd never had a fuss made about any birthday when she was a child. I could sympathize with that, I'd never had much of a birthday myself as a kid.'

He closed his eyes briefly. 'I wanted it all to be perfect. I was going to tie a satin ribbon round the steering-wheel, with a big bow. I was looking forward to seeing her face.'

He appeared on the verge of tears but recovered himself after a moment.

'I was in Blakestone on a call one day and I spotted the garage, I saw it was empty. I'd been keeping my eyes open as I went about. I went up to the house and spoke to the old lady. She was very pleased for me to rent it, she was glad of the money. It was handy enough—and it had water and electricity laid on, that was a big plus.'

'Where is this car now?'

'I sold it to a garage.' He thought back. 'Monday, last week, that would be. It went clean out of my head at first, after what had happened. I remembered it again when it was coming up to Anna's birthday. I'd only got the garage till the end of October, I realized I'd have to do something about the car.' He gave Kelsey the address of the garage where he'd sold it.

On the way back to Cannonbridge the Chief called in on Dr Peake who was just finishing evening surgery.

Yes, the doctor clearly recalled his conversation with Conway about a car for Anna. Yes, he had suggested Conway should teach Anna to drive, buy her a small car if he could afford it.

It also came back to Peake that he had advised Conway always to present any new enterprise to Anna as a *fait accompli*, not discuss it with her beforehand, not give her the chance to think up objections, worry herself into a state of nerves.

CHAPTER 20

The garage where Conway had sold the car lay some twenty-five miles from Cannonbridge on the Northcott road. On Thursday morning Sergeant Lambert drove Chief Inspector Kelsey over there.

The garage owner was friendly and cooperative. Yes, he

had bought a car from Conway some ten days ago. He didn't need to look it up in his records, the transaction was fresh in his mind, principally because of the excellent condition of the car but also because no more than fifteen minutes ago he had let an eighteen-year-old girl, the daughter of a neighbour, take the car out on a trial run, with her father sitting beside her.

The garage owner had paid a good price for the car. He had inquired why Conway was selling it so soon after buying it and was told the car had been bought on behalf of another person who now no longer needed it.

The Chief asked if the car's performance had been enhanced beyond normal limits and was told no. There had been no souping up, no engine replacement, no fitting of twin carburettors, nothing like that. Nor had one iota of safety been sacrificed to a desire for speed.

Kelsey told the owner that he wished to take temporary possession of the vehicle. Every care would be taken, it would be returned by noon the following day. He was offered no objection.

'There's the car coming back now!' the owner exclaimed. Kelsey turned his head and watched it drive on to the forecourt. A nippy little vehicle a few years old. A make renowned for reliability and workmanlike qualities, not marketed on fashion or fancy gimmicks. An unobtrusive outline, colour a muted shade of grey-green.

The girl and her father stepped out of the car. It was clear from their expressions that they had decided to buy it. The father was already taking out his cheque-book. 'First-class,' he reported with a broad smile. 'A cracking little car.'

The garage owner began to explain why the Chief was here. The delighted look vanished from the girl's face. But a measured dose of the Chief's particular mixture of soothing syrup and soft soap soon persuaded the pair to accept the brief delay with a good grace.

When they had departed the garage owner handed the

keys to Kelsey before taking himself off to deal with another customer.

Lambert glanced at the Chief, expecting him to say which of them was driving what car back to Cannonbridge where the Chief had a number of appointments waiting for him. But Kelsey stood lost in thought, staring up the road.

'We're nearly half way to Northcott,' he said after some moments. 'That woman Mrs Ackroyd mentioned—the coal merchant's daughter, the one who set her cap at Conway.'

'Joyce Kimbolt,' Lambert supplied, with his ever-reliable memory for names.

'That's the one. She lives in Northcott. Or just outside.' The Chief's craggy features took on a brooding look. 'She'd be altogether a bigger fish for Conway to land, if he could manage to hook her. If it hadn't been for her dad sticking his oar in, she might very well have married Conway. It could have been her ashes scattered in a garden of remembrance, not Anna's.'

He gazed reflectively at Lambert. 'Her father's not around any more. Died six months ago, Ackroyd said. Wouldn't do any harm for you to nip over to Northcott now, see if you can manage a word with Miss Kimbolt. I'll take Anna's car back to Cannonbridge.'

As Lambert drove into the outskirts of Northcott another fact Ackroyd had let drop bobbed up in his brain: Joyce Kimbolt had put her house up for sale. Might come in handy, that, he could pass himself off as a potential purchaser. Just as well he was on his own. Miss Kimbolt might be willing to swallow one hefty guy in a dark suit and white shirt turning up out of the blue to take a look at the property but two of them together spelled coppers in anyone's books.

He had no difficulty in discovering—via the phone book and an obliging passer-by—where the house was situated. A little way out the other side of town, in pleasantly rural surroundings. But as he came in sight of the dwelling he saw, on the estate agent's board, a diagonal sticker triumphantly proclaiming the proud boast: SOLD.

Nevertheless he parked the police car discreetly out of sight and walked round to the house, an exuberant specimen of Victorian Gothic.

In her spacious bedroom on the first floor Joyce Kimbolt was assessing the array of garments on her bed, the fruits of her morning's shopping. Her expression hovered between anxiety and pleasure as she surveyed, considered, picked up and set down.

She crossed to a wardrobe and rattled the hangers along the rail, frowning, pondering. She plucked several items down and flung them over a chair, on their way to a charity shop.

She returned to the bed and looked at her purchases again. She carried a dress over to a long mirror by the window and held it up against her. Her image gazed critically back at her. Indisputably plain, irredeemably bony, neither elegance nor grace.

Her ear caught the crunch of footsteps on the gravel below. She moved to one side of the window and looked down.

A tall, broad-shouldered man was standing a few yards away with his back to her, glancing about. Come to view the property, no doubt. He'd notice the sticker in a moment, take himself off. He turned to survey the house and she saw that he was youngish, rather good-looking.

She smiled and darted back to the bed, laid the dress down. She cast a hasty look in the glass, primped her hair, assumed a bright expression. She plunged from the room and down the stairs with ungainly speed.

Still no ring from the bell. She threw open the door. He was still there, he turned at the sound.

'Did you want to see the house?' she called, a little breathless. Her manner was archly girlish. She stepped outside.

He made an apologetic gesture as he came over. 'I'm sorry to have disturbed you. I see by the board the house has been sold.'

She nodded. 'Yes. I'm moving out very soon.'

'It would be much too big for me, anyway,' he admitted. 'And way out of my reach financially, I've no doubt. But I couldn't resist taking a look. It's a magnificent property. Highly individual.'

She grimaced. 'I think it's hideous.' She giggled. Her upper lip rode above long teeth, disclosing an unlovely expanse of gum. 'I can say that, now it's sold.' She gave him an all-embracing glance. 'You're not from round here?'

He shook his head. 'I live a good sixty miles away.'

'The house has been bought by a developer. He's going to turn it into flats, and build another four flats in the garden.' She smiled. 'You could always come back and take a look at the flats if you're not suited by the time they're built.' She drifted off with Lambert on a tour of the exterior, pointing out particularly extravagant features.

'I'll be glad to be out of it,' she confided. 'I've never liked it.'

'I imagine you'll be moving somewhere smaller?' Lambert hazarded.

'I haven't bought another house.' She spoke with the relaxed freedom of someone who knows she will never again clap eyes on her listener. 'I'm off to France, to start with.' Her voice took on an edge of excitement. 'I've rented a villa while we have a scout round. We're going into the property business in Europe, my partner and me.

'My partner's gone into it all thoroughly, he's a business-man. He says there's terrific scope for holiday homes over there. Folk from this country would jump at them. France, Spain, Italy—even Turkey. He says property's still dirt cheap in Turkey. Lovely old farmhouses and cottages, crying out to be modernized.'

'It sounds very exciting.'

'Oh, it is!' She clasped her hands together. 'It's only been settled between us quite recently. Sometimes when I wake up in the mornings I still can't credit it isn't all just a wonderful dream.' She tilted her head. 'Funny how things work out. I was sure my father would live to be a hundred just to spite me, I'd be an old woman by the time he died, too old for any life of my own.'

Her voice dropped to a confidential level. 'This partner I mentioned, he's more than a partner, actually. We're getting married the moment he's free. We have to lie low for the present till his divorce comes through, he doesn't want any hitches or complications. I knew him before, a year or two back, when my father was alive.'

She pulled a face. 'My father never wanted me to marry anyone, so nothing came of it and he went away.' She smiled. 'But then he heard my father had died and he got in touch with me again. I could hardly believe it, I was sure I'd never see him again. I thought we could get married right away but he told me we couldn't, not just yet awhile. And do you know what the reason was?' She looked earnestly up at Lambert. 'He was so upset when he was telling me about it, he could hardly get the words out.'

Her voice was full of drama. 'He'd gone and got himself married! I must admit I cried when he told me, I was absolutely shattered. He'd got married on the rebound, he'd been so miserable over me.'

She waved a hand. 'Of course the marriage was a total disaster. But he still won't talk about her. All he'll say is it was a stupid mistake on both sides, nobody's fault, they just weren't suited.' Her eyes glowed. 'It gives you a lovely warm feeling of security, knowing a man's got that kind of loyalty, even to a woman he never really loved, you've got to admire him. It makes you feel you could trust him through thick and thin.'

She made a little face. 'I don't know anything at all about his wife, I don't know her name or how old she is. I don't even know where he's living now, he wouldn't tell me. He says it's in my own interests not to know anything at all.

I'm to be kept clear of everything till it's all over, he's not having me dragged into it at any price. He won't risk anything going wrong this time, now we've found each other again.'

She widened her eyes at Lambert. 'I can't even get in touch with him, I always have to wait for him to get in touch with me. Still, it makes it all the more romantic and exciting.'

She giggled, like a mischievous child. 'I did say to him I could always look through all the different phone books till I found his name and address, but he said he's not been living where he is now long enough to have his name in the book.' She giggled again. 'And in any case, it's not an unusual name, I'd never be able to tell which—'

She broke off and clapped a hand to her mouth. She simpered archly up at him. 'Silly me! I nearly said what his name was, just then. That would never do!'

On the way back to Cannonbridge Lambert stopped at a roadside box to ring Zodiac Soft Furnishings. The girl at the other end of the phone had a cheerful, friendly voice.

'I'd like to get in touch with your Mr David Conway,' Lambert told her. 'I wondered if you could give me his phone number.'

'Certainly,' she said at once. 'I'll look it up.' She supplied the number a minute or two later. 'But he's not our Mr Conway any more,' she informed him. 'Or he won't be after tomorrow.'

'How's that?' Lambert asked.

'He's leaving. Tomorrow's his last day with Zodiac.'

'That's a bit sudden, isn't it?'

'Depends what you mean by sudden. He wasn't here long, I grant you that, but he's not leaving on the spur of the moment, there hasn't been a bust-up or anything like that—not so far as I know. He gave in his notice, all right and proper, four weeks ago. I must say, though, I was surprised myself when I heard he'd given in his notice—it was my friend in the personnel office that told me. Personal reasons, so Mr Conway said, that's what she told me. Everyone here will be sorry to see him go. He was well liked, he got on well with everybody.'

Her voice took on a matey note. 'Between you and me, I expect he's had a better offer elsewhere, only he isn't letting on. Can't say I blame him, if that's what the truth of it is, you've got to look after number one in this life. Other firms are always trying to poach good salesmen and they say Mr Conway's a first-class salesman, one of the best.'

She suddenly bethought herself of her duty to Zodiac. 'If it's loose covers or soft furnishings you were wanting to talk to Mr Conway about, we've got a new man starting in his place on Monday. I haven't met him yet myself but I'm sure he'll be very good. He'll look after you very well, you won't have any complaints.'

When Lambert got back to the police station the Chief was in conference. Lambert immediately set about phoning every estate agent in the town with a view to discovering which of them handled the letting of Ferndale.

At his fourth call he struck lucky. He asked if the manager could see him and was told yes, if he came round right away. Ten minutes later he was sitting in the manager's office.

'Mr Conway took Ferndale on a shorthold tenancy,' the manager told him. 'For six months initially, with an option to extend by the month. The six months were up on August 31st.' Conway had extended for September and again for October. At the end of October Conway asked if it was possible to extend for another two weeks only. He wanted to be out of Ferndale as soon as possible, after the tragic death of his wife. 'Can't blame him,' the manager said. 'It must be a nightmare staying on there alone after a terrible thing like that. I know I wouldn't care to do it.'

He spread his hands. 'In the ordinary way, of course, we don't deal in parts of months, but it so happens that I have

a client who sold his house through us and bought another—
not through us, I may say, or I hope we'd have managed
things a bit better. He got himself into a bit of a fix, didn't
get his dates properly synchronized. He has to be out of his
old house by November 15th and can't get possession of the
new house till December 1st. He was in one hell of a stew.
Family man, the prospect of no roof over their heads, wife
playing merry hell, you can imagine.'

'I told him about Ferndale and he jumped at it. It'll tide
him over nicely.' He dropped his voice. 'He doesn't seem
to know what happened to poor Mrs Conway, he's certainly
never mentioned it to me. I only knew about it myself
because of Mr Conway getting on to us about the lease. If
it was in the paper I never came across it.'

He twirled his pen. 'I don't propose to enlighten my
client. What he and his lady wife don't know won't hurt
them and if they do by any chance find out while they're at
Ferndale, the two weeks will be up before they've had time
to digest it.'

He leaned back in his chair. 'So I got back to Mr Conway
and told him yes, he could extend for the first two weeks in
November.'

'He'll be leaving on the fourteenth, then?' Lambert said.
Five days' time.

The manager shrugged. 'That's up to him. He's paid the
rent till the fourteenth but of course he's free to go before
if he wants to, as long as he hands in the keys and leaves
the place in good order.'

He waved a hand. 'Not that we've any worries on that
score, he's been a first-class tenant. I only wish they were
all like Mr Conway. And the inventory's already been done.
He rang to ask if we could get that out of the way, in case
he did want to go early, so we did it on Tuesday. No trouble
with it, everything satisfactory. Mr Conway can leave any
time he wants.'

CHAPTER 21

When Chief Inspector Kelsey returned to the Cannonbridge
police station from the garage on Thursday morning,
he passed Anna's car over to the best police driver he
could lay hands on, instructing him to take it out and drive
it, get to know the vehicle, hold himself ready early next
morning to carry out in it a timed run over the ground the
Chief had by now more than half convinced himself
Conway must have covered in the car on the morning of
October 23rd.

True, conditions wouldn't be in every particular precisely
parallel. It would be a Friday and not a Monday, traffic
would very probably be different. The light, as well as the
weather, must have altered after the lapse of eighteen
days—apart from the change in light conditions brought
about by the ending of British Summer Time on October
29th. But it would be a reasonably close approximation, it
would serve well enough.

The Chief pored over a detailed map of the terrain with
the driver beside him. Between them they decided on the
most likely route for Conway to have chosen: by no means
the most straightforward route but the quietest and least
observed, where the little grey-green car—a vehicle no
acquaintance of Conway's, chancing to spy it at that hour,
would in any way connect with Conway—could whisk
unobtrusively along the lanes and side roads.

The driver was to proceed throughout as quickly as was
compatible with safety and the rule of law, bearing in mind
at all times the need to avoid—as Conway would have had
to avoid—drawing any attention to himself, whether driving
or on foot.

He should drive first to Mrs Egan's garage and lock
Anna's car away inside. He was then to take himself off on

foot to Blakestone station to await the arrival of the steam train that left Oldmoor at 7.32.

The timing would begin the moment the first passenger stepped down from the train. The police driver would then at once return on foot to Mrs Egan's garage, take out Anna's car, lock the garage again and set off in the car for Ferndale.

He should park for a moment under the trees at the rear of the bungalow, then start the engine up again and drive to Sedgefield Junction, leave the vehicle in the station car park and get to the departure platform as quickly as possible. No need to allow for any stop at the booking office—Conway could have bought his ticket for Dunstall in advance.

On Thursday evening the Chief had a test of his own to carry out. Ideally it should have been carried out at Ferndale but as he could scarcely expect Conway to be obliging enough to permit such an operation he had to make do instead with his own flat, carefully mimicking and timing what he imagined Conway's sequence of actions to have been if he had indeed returned to the bungalow that Monday morning.

From a painstaking reconstruction, three times repeated, the Chief finally arrived at a considered estimate of seventeen minutes as the time it would have taken Conway to deal with all he would have had to do between stepping out of Anna's car at the rear of Ferndale and getting back into the car again to drive to Sedgefield Junction.

Early on Friday morning, some time after the police driver had set off on his mission, Sergeant Lambert drove the Chief to Sedgefield Junction. At ten minutes past eight they positioned themselves on the platform from which the 8.50 would leave for Dunstall.

The Chief was devoured by restlessness. He paced about, glancing endlessly at his watch, waiting for the police driver to show up. The gap between the moment of the driver's arrival and the departure of the Dunstall train would indi-

cate the length of time available to Conway to carry out all
that had to be done at Ferndale. If the gap was less than
seventeen minutes, then that was the end of it, the Chief
had incontestably been barking up the wrong tree, Conway
could have had no hand in Anna's death.

But if the gap was longer than seventeen minutes, while
it certainly wouldn't mean Conway had definitely murdered
Anna, it would at least place the murder within the bounds
of possibility.

At long last the police driver appeared in sight. As he
came up to where they stood on the platform Kelsey's watch
showed 8.28.

The Chief drew a long, wavering breath. 'Twenty-two
minutes,' he said to Lambert. 'Conway could have done it
with five minutes to spare.'

On the way back to Cannonbridge they turned off for
Blakestone village. They called again at the cottage occupied
by the retired couple who worked for Mrs Egan. This time
they were lucky enough to catch Mrs Yealland on the point
of setting off to another of her little domestic jobs. Her
husband was out, gone into town. He wouldn't be back till
around three o'clock.

'Nothing for either of you to worry about,' the Chief
assured Mrs Yealland. 'Nothing that in any way concerns
your husband personally. It's just that we think he might
be in a position to help us with some information.'

She was intrigued. Certainly they could call back in the
afternoon, she was sure her husband would be glad to assist
the police in any way he could. 'Better make it half past
three,' she advised. 'To be on the safe side.'

And when they returned at three-thirty Yealland was on
the look-out for them in his trim front garden, occupying
his time while waiting by giving an extra rub to windows
already gleaming. As soon as he saw the car he set down his
wash-leather and went to meet them. A brawny, grey-haired
man with a stubborn chin and an observant eye.

He took them into the kitchen, sat them down, made them tea. There was no sign of his wife.

'I understand from Mrs Egan,' the Chief began, 'that she let her garage recently to a businessman.'

'That's right,' Yealland confirmed. 'She told me you'd been to see her about it.'

No, he had never spoken to the businessman, never laid eyes on him.

Had he ever seen the car that was kept in the garage?

He gave an energetic nod. 'Oh yes, I saw it all right, I saw it several times. I go by the garage every day, twice at least, often more. When Mrs Egan told me she'd rented the garage I stopped by on my way home a day or two later and had a look in.'

'What colour was the car?'

'It was a greyish green.'

'Was the car ever moved from the garage as far as you know?'

Yealland gave another vigorous nod. 'Yes, it was. After that first time I always had a look in when I went by. Three or four times I saw a different car inside.'

Kelsey sat up.

'I had a look at that, as well. It was bigger than the green car, beige colour.'

'What time of day did you see this beige car in the garage?'

'It was there different times of day, sometimes morning, sometimes afternoon, but it was never there very long. I'd see it there and then next time I went by it would be gone and the green car would be back inside again.' Making dummy runs over the route, the Chief told himself; Conway would have to get his timing spot on.

'Sometimes the garage would be empty,' Yealland added. 'No car around at all. Then, next time I went by, the green car would be back again.' He frowned in thought. 'There was one time when the garage stayed empty for a day or two and I didn't see any car about at all.'

'Can you remember exactly when that was?'

Yealland tilted his head back and closed his eyes. 'I went past the garage on the Sunday afternoon and the green car was inside. I went past again first thing on the Monday morning and the green car was gone. The garage was empty, the doors were closed. There was no other car anywhere about.

'It was still like that on the Tuesday and again on the Wednesday morning, but when I went by on the Wednesday afternoon I saw the green car back inside again. It was there every day after that till the let was up.'

'Can you remember which Monday this was?'

Yealland grinned. 'That I can. I'd borrowed some tools on the Saturday dinner-time from a chap in the village— carpenter, he is. We were expecting my wife's brother and sister-in-law a few days later, they were stopping the night with us on their way to the airport, they were off to Majorca for a holiday.'

He made a face. 'This sister-in-law thinks a mighty lot of herself. My missus always gets in one hell of a flap whenever she knows they're coming. They rang up on the Friday evening to say they'd be here the following Wednesday. The minute my missus put the phone down she was off round the house like a whippet, giving everything the once-over, to see if it would be good enough for her ladyship.

'She'd been on at me long enough to do something about the kitchen units. I must admit they were getting a bit the worse for wear. She said I'd got to do something about them pronto, no more excuses. So we went into town on the Saturday morning and bought some new doors for the units and one or two new worktops. I spent the rest of the weekend fitting them. This carpenter chap, he only let me have the tools if I swore black and blue he'd have them back on the Monday morning before half past eight.'

He went across to a wall calendar. 'That's the Monday the garage was empty.' He jabbed a finger at the date. 'October 23rd.'

CHAPTER 22

'You're positive about that?' Kelsey pressed him.

'No doubt at all. The brother and sister-in-law stopped with us the Wednesday night, October 25th.' He jabbed again. 'The missus marked it down here on the calendar. You can see for yourself.'

Kelsey went over and saw a black-ink ring encircling the 25th. 'Can you say what time it was when you went by the garage that Monday morning and noticed it was empty?' he asked.

'I can tell you that, too,' Yealland responded with certainty. 'I walked up the village to give the carpenter back his tools. It was twenty-five past eight when I got to his house.' He grinned again. 'I know that because he looked at his watch when he saw me. He'd just driven his van out of the garage. He called over: '"Twenty-five past eight! You believe in cutting it fine!"'

Yealland pondered. 'I reckon that would make it around a quarter past eight when I went by the garage.'

'Did you see the beige car anywhere near the garage at any time that Monday morning?'

Yealland shook his head. 'No, there was no sign of it that morning. Or of any other car anywhere about.'

The road back to Cannonbridge took them close to the Garbutts' smallholding. As Lambert halted for a junction the Chief's eye was caught by a sign above the hedge offering an array of produce from goose eggs to cut flowers.

'We'll call in there,' he told Lambert. 'I'll get some flowers or a plant for my cleaning woman, she's at home with 'flu.' He could take his offering along over the weekend, it might help to speed her return to work.

They found Irene Garbutt over by the greenhouses, dispatching the last of the outdoor jobs in the fading light. She was delighted to welcome them in the role of customers.

After some discussion the Chief selected a superb scarlet begonia full of buds. Lambert bought a jar of honey for his landlady, on the well-tried principle of keeping sweet the female ruling the household of which he was currently a member.

'It's good to see you looking more cheerful,' Kelsey told Mrs Garbutt as he paid for the begonia.

'I'm coming to terms with what's happened,' she agreed. 'That doesn't mean I've completely forgiven myself for not realizing something was terribly wrong with poor Anna. It'll be a lesson I'll never forget. A young life like that and I stood by and let it slip away.'

'You're too hard on yourself,' the Chief told her. 'You did your best to be friendly. You couldn't force Anna to respond if she didn't want to.'

'That's what Bob keeps telling me. After she got ill I called in now and then but she was never comfortable with me. I asked her once or twice if she'd like to come out with me on my rounds, or maybe I could drop her off in Cannonbridge so she could do a bit of shopping while I made my deliveries, I'd pick her up again afterwards. But I could never persuade her.'

She looked up at Kelsey. 'I did get her to go to church with me one Sunday, though.'

'When was that?'

'Early June, it would be. I stopped by Ferndale one afternoon. I could see she'd been crying. I tried to get her to talk about what was upsetting her but she wouldn't open up. I said—on the spur of the moment—if there was something troubling her and she'd like to get it off her chest, why not talk to the vicar? Laidlaw, his name was. He's retired now, but he was a lovely man, so kind and understanding, very good with young folk. And you could guarantee nothing you said would ever go any further. I made a point of telling her that.

'She did seem interested but she said she couldn't ask David to take her to church, he wasn't a churchgoer, never had been. And he liked to go along and give a hand on the steam railway on Sundays. I told her she could come with me. And she did come, the next Sunday—that was the only time she came, I could never persuade her again. But she did quite like it, I could see she did.

'The vicar was just coming up to retirement, it was his last Sunday at Oldmoor church—there are five parishes in the living. He preached a beautiful farewell sermon, I saw some of the older folk wiping their eyes. Anna listened to every word, she kept her eyes glued on him the whole time. At the end he said he'd put his new address up on the notice board in the porch and anyone who cared to call in to see him would always be welcome.

'When you come out of church the vicar always stands by the door to have a word with you as you go by but Anna wouldn't stop to be introduced, she went hurrying on.'

She wrote down Laidlaw's present address for the Chief, in a village twenty miles away.

Darkness had fallen by the time they reached the village where the Reverend Mr Laidlaw was enjoying his retirement. Light shone from his cottage.

As Lambert halted the car a middle-aged woman in outdoor clothes let herself out of the front door and walked down the path to the gate. She looked inquiringly at them. Kelsey got out and approached her. She was a pleasant-spoken woman with a helpful manner.

Yes, Mr Laidlaw was in. She was his housekeeper. She lived in the village, came in daily. She was sure Mr Laidlaw would spare time to see them, though he was busy packing for his holiday. He was off first thing in the morning, flying to Guernsey to stay with his married daughter and her family. 'It'll do him the world of good,' she declared. 'He was very off-colour earlier this week but he seems a lot better now, thank goodness.'

At the sound of the doorbell Laidlaw came down from his bedroom. A rotund little man, rosy-cheeked and silver-haired, with a benign, fatherly countenance.

Kelsey explained who he was, and that he thought the vicar might be able to help them. Yes, certainly, Laidlaw would be happy to talk to them. He took them inside and sat them down, tried to press refreshments on them but the Chief wouldn't put him to the trouble.

Kelsey began by asking if a Mrs Anna Conway had been to see the clergyman at some time in the last few months.

'Conway?' Laidlaw wrinkled his brow. 'I can't recall anyone of that name.'

'About twenty years old,' Kelsey enlarged. 'Thin, nervy.'

'Now that does begin to ring a bell,' Laidlaw said after a moment. 'Yes, there was a young woman. Her name was Anna, right enough, but not Conway.' He glanced about. 'What was it? I do know.' He suddenly snapped his fingers. 'Newby! Mrs Anna Newby!'

'That's the one,' Kelsey said. 'Newby was her maiden name. When did she come to see you?'

Laidlaw shook his head regretfully. 'I'm sorry, but I'm afraid I can't tell you anything more. She came to see me in the strictest confidence. She made a particular point of that. I gave her my word.'

'Anna Conway's dead,' Kelsey told him. He outlined briefly the circumstances of her death. 'We're looking into it. One of the things we're trying to determine is the state of her mind. We thought you might be able to throw some light on that.'

Laidlaw had listened in growing distress. 'What an appalling thing to have happened!' he exclaimed. 'What a terrible waste of a young life.' He was silent for a moment. 'But I can't say I'm altogether surprised she took her own life. She was in a pretty bad state when I saw her.' He looked up at the Chief. 'This alters things, of course. I'll be glad to help in any way I can.'

Kelsey asked him again when Anna had come to see him.

'I only saw her the one time. It was a week or two after I retired and came here to live,' Laidlaw recalled. 'She phoned one afternoon and asked if she could come over to see me. She sounded very tense and agitated. She gave me her name, Mrs Anna Newby, the name meant nothing to me. She didn't give any address. We fixed a time for the following morning.

'She was so screwed up with nerves when she arrived she could hardly get a word out. I gave her some tea and after a bit she loosened up a little.'

'What did she want to talk to you about?'

'Once she got going there was no stopping her. It all came pouring out as if she'd been dying to say it all to someone, anyone. I'm sure that was what she needed as much as anything, simply to unburden herself to someone she need never see again.'

'What was it all about?'

'It was pretty tangled and confused. She'd obviously been mulling things over for some time, trying to figure out every aspect, every implication, of what was bothering her— enough to make anyone's head reel. Of course, all she'd managed to do was get herself into a complete muddle where she could hardly tell fact from fantasy, right from wrong, any more.

'I tried to get her to give me some solid facts to go on, I tried asking her direct questions, but she wasn't having that, she shied away at once.'

'Did you manage to get any picture of what the trouble was?'

'Yes, I did get a picture of sorts but I wouldn't like to say how accurate it is. There seemed to be two things tormenting her, separate but connected. The first was that she was blaming herself for the death of someone close to her, someone she'd been fond of. I gathered some kind of accident had happened and she felt she had failed in her duty of care towards this person in allowing the accident to happen. She should have been able to foresee the possibility of an accident and taken steps to prevent it.

'I asked her if other people—particularly any authorities involved—had in any way blamed her for what had happened but she said no, far from it, everyone had been very kind and sympathetic, but that hadn't made her feel any better.

'I couldn't see there was likely to be anything much in all this breast-beating. It seemed to me she was displaying all the signs of someone who hadn't been able to come to terms with bereavement, could scarcely bear to think of it, to credit it had really happened.' That figures, Kelsey thought. In her drawstring bag of hidden treasures she'd kept the certificate of her marriage to Reardon, kept the wedding ring he'd given her, but she hadn't kept his death certificate there, that irrefutable piece of evidence that he really had died an agonizing death.

Laidlaw spread his hands. 'Grief, guilt, depression, agitation, all the classic symptoms. Most folk get through by talking things out with a good friend or relative but some—like Anna Conway—need professional help before they can get back on an even keel.'

He shook his head. 'Not something for the well-meaning amateur psychiatrist to tackle. Could end up making things a good deal worse.'

'Did you feel you could offer her any advice?'

'I asked her if she'd talked over any of this with her husband. I was fishing, really. I was expecting her to say at once that she couldn't talk to him, he was dead. I guessed it was the death of her husband that was at the root of it.' He gestured. 'But I was wrong, she wasn't a widow. She said she couldn't talk to her husband about it, she daren't talk to him about it.' He levelled a look at the Chief. 'That seemed to be the second matter that was troubling her, her suspicions of her husband.'

'Suspicions?' Kelsey echoed.

Laidlaw nodded. 'That's what they amounted to. She

was no longer sure how much she could trust him.' He flung out a hand. 'But there again, whether or not it was all just overheated imaginings, I have no idea.'

'What did she have to say about her husband?'

'She said she loved him, he was more important to her than anyone else in the world, she'd loved him from the first day they'd met. She'd always trusted him completely— until quite recently. There was nothing she wanted more than to be able to trust him completely again, go on trusting him, so she could be wholeheartedly happy with him, the way she'd hoped they'd be when she married him.

'But terrible thoughts had started coming into her head. They were wearing her out, destroying her peace of mind. She knew she was in a nervy state, she was almost certain the thoughts were entirely the result of that, there was no truth in them at all.'

'Did she say what kind of thoughts they were?'

'Thoughts that she might be foolish to trust her husband, that things might not be what she had believed them to be. That the death of this person she'd been fond of might not have been entirely accidental, that maybe her husband had had a hand in it. And—this seemed to be her worst anxiety—that maybe she herself in all innocence had made it possible for her husband to have a hand in that death.

'She'd struggled against these thoughts, done her best to dismiss them. They made her feel ill and panicky, disloyal and treacherous, frightened of her own shadow. But she couldn't get rid of them, they kept on returning stronger than ever, they'd started turning up, one way or another, in her dreams, so she was afraid to go to sleep.

'She felt it was out of the question to say anything of all this to her husband. She was almost certain if she did speak to him that he would be able to convince her it was nothing more than sick fancies, there wasn't a shred of truth in any of her fears—but once he knew what appalling things had been going on inside her head, there could be no going back, no unsaying what had been said. How could he ever feel

the same way about her again? She would have destroyed
the whole basis of loving trust between them. He would
always be thinking: What motive is she imputing to me
now? He could never feel the same way about her again.
Things could never again be the same between them, in the
end it would split them for good.

'That would leave her totally alone in the world, she had
no one else at all. She couldn't face that, it was the worst
thing she could imagine. Anything would be better than
that. Even death.'

CHAPTER 23

'What did you advise her?'

'The first thing I tried to do was ease her anxieties. I
explained that bereavement can play strange tricks on the
mind, that her case wasn't unusual, in my years as a
priest I'd often come across folk who harboured all sorts of
unwarranted doubts and guilts after the sudden death of
someone very close. Suspicions, too, every kind of fanciful
suspicion. That seemed to relieve her a good deal.

'I asked her if other people, especially anyone in authority,
had ever suggested her husband might have had anything
to do with the death of this person she'd been fond of.
She said no, there had never been the slightest suggestion
of it. Then again, when she was obliged to say that out
loud to someone else, she did look very relieved, as if she
was being forced to face reality instead of conjuring up
fantasies.'

'You did feel the whole thing was fanciful? There was no
basis of reality in any of it?'

Laidlaw shook his head at once. 'No, I'm not saying that
at all. I had no conceivable way of knowing if there was
anything in it or not. I had no intention of getting tangled
up in all that, I didn't see it as my territory. I was sure the

best thing I could do for her was put her in touch with professional help.

'I asked her if she'd seen a doctor. She said she hadn't, she hadn't been to a doctor for years, she wasn't on any doctor's books. I said that didn't matter in the slightest, she could go and see any doctor, any one of them would be only too willing to help her. She'd be dealt with in complete confidence, she needn't say any more than she wanted to, but a doctor could at least see she had something to steady her nerves, give her a good night's sleep, bring her appetite back. That might be all she needed to start seeing things in a better light again, get everything back into proportion.'

He darted a shrewd look at Kelsey. 'I was pretty sure any doctor she talked to would steer her towards a psychiatrist but I didn't tell her that or she wouldn't go near a doctor at all. Folk in that state are usually terrified at the notion of being referred to a psychiatrist, they're sure they'll end up in a mental ward.

'It took a bit of persuasion but I did get her to promise me faithfully she would see a doctor very soon. Once she'd promised, that seemed to be the end of it. She looked more relaxed, she even smiled, as if she was pleased she'd been jockeyed into making some kind of decision. She stood up and thanked me. She said she had to get off to catch her bus.'

He came with them to the door when they left. The Chief thanked him warmly for his help, apologized for keeping him from his packing, hoped he would enjoy his holiday in Guernsey.

'I'm really looking forward to it,' Laidlaw told them with lively pleasure. 'Nothing like a good dose of sea air before the winter, always does my chest and sinuses a power of good. I was afraid I might have to postpone my jaunt. I woke up a few days ago with a nasty sore throat. That usually means I'm in for a bad cold—and I couldn't risk inflicting that on my grandchildren, the baby's only a few months old, colds can be a serious matter at that age.'

He gave a broad smile. 'But I've been gargling and inhaling and drinking herb tea—along with a good tot of hot whisky and lemon at bedtime. Between them they seem to have done the trick. I feel as right as rain now.'

'That's good,' Kelsey said heartily. 'It's always disappointing to have to cancel a holiday at the last moment.'

'It certainly is. And with commercial holidays, of course, there's a stiff financial penalty to pay as well.'

Kelsey froze to the spot. He felt the hair prickle along his scalp.

Laidlaw went on chatting for another minute or two, then he said goodbye and the two policemen went off down the path. Kelsey halted by the car door.

'That cruise Anna Conway was going on,' he said to Lambert. 'Do you know the name of the travel firm the cruise was booked through?'

'I did see the name.' Lambert stood frowning in thought. After a few moments his brain obediently flung up an image of the glossy shipping-line brochure with the name of the travel agent stamped across it in scarlet. Below the name, a scarlet logo: the stereotyped outline of a bird in flight.

'Falcon!' he declared in triumph. 'Falcon Travel!' Not one of the big countrywide firms but sizable enough, a regional concern with several branches in the county.

'Do you know which branch of Falcon?' Kelsey asked.

But Lambert could only shake his head. His brain sent up no further word.

The Chief consulted his watch. Three minutes to six. He turned and went rapidly back to the house. He pressed the bell.

'I'm sorry to trouble you again,' he said when Laidlaw had once again descended from his bedroom. 'May I use your phone?'

He had to look up the number of the Falcon head office. By the time he had tapped out the digits and heard the double ring begin, the minute hand of his watch had slipped past the hour.

All he got was a recorded voice asking him to leave a message. The office was now closed, it wouldn't be open again until eight o'clock next morning.

At ten-thirty the Chief was assailed by a prolonged fit of yawning and decided to take himself off to bed. He had spent a restless evening in front of the television, intermittently plagued by the notion that Conway might be about to slip the net, clear off to Europe—hell's delight trying to catch up with him again.

He got into bed and stretched out a hand to extinguish the bedside lamp. As his fingers touched the switch the nagging thought abruptly returned, now in the form of a question, even more alarming: Had Conway already slipped the net?

He sprang out of bed and went at a rush into the living-room, snatched up the phone and tapped out the Ferndale number. He heard the rings begin. And continue. Unanswered.

That's it, he told himself in bleak dismay. He's cut and run. He felt an iron fist clutch at his vitals.

All at once a voice, Conway's voice, spoke at the other end, weary and patient, giving his number.

The Chief closed his eyes in a flood of relief. He replaced the receiver without a word and went back to bed—now, perhaps, with some hope of sleep.

Kelsey was up early. He was in his office, sitting tensely by the phone, before eight. As the wall clock showed the hour he lifted the receiver.

Falcon Travel didn't let him down. A live female voice, crisply efficient, answered him. In no time at all, by courtesy of the Falcon computer, he had the address of the branch that had handled the booking of Anna Conway's cruise; it was in a town some thirty miles away.

Five minutes later Kelsey was sitting in the passenger seat as Sergeant Lambert edged the car out of the forecourt.

Traffic was already building up. It was over an hour before they arrived at their destination.

The Falcon branch was situated in the main shopping street. On the pavement outside, a woman was selling poppies in remembrance of wars long past. November was never the busiest of times in the travel trade, even on a Saturday morning, and there was as yet only a trickle of customers inside the bright, modern premises.

The Chief asked to speak to the manager but was told he was out, he wouldn't be back before midday. In that case, the Chief explained, he would like to speak to whichever member of staff had dealt with the cruise booking. A few minutes later the two policemen were seated in a side office, talking to a female assistant.

The booking had been made on September 12th. The assistant recalled it clearly, chiefly because of the great care Mr Conway had taken over it. He had explained the state of his wife's health, had been very concerned about her, had taken great pains to make sure he decided on the right cruise.

He was particularly insistent that there should be first-class medical attention available so that he could send his wife off with an easy mind. He had paid in full, there and then. It wasn't one of their five-star luxury cruises, but expensive enough.

The Chief asked in what circumstances the booking had been cancelled but the assistant knew nothing of any cancellation. She had assumed Mrs Conway was at this moment aboard the cruise ship.

'You'll have to speak to the manager about that,' she told Kelsey. It was a cast-iron rule in the branch that all customers with cancellation on their minds must be referred to the manager. He prided himself—with justification—on being able to persuade a good proportion of them that what they really needed was not cancellation but some revision of the original plan: an earlier or later booking, cheaper or dearer hotel, quieter or livelier resort.

Could the assistant recall if Mr Conway had taken out any cancellation insurance?

The assistant's memory was very clear on that point as Mr Conway had discussed it with her at some length. She had outlined for him the various circumstances in which the insurance company would or would not pay out.

'In the end he decided against insurance,' she told the Chief. He was sure the cruise wouldn't be cancelled but if it were, the most likely reason would be that his wife had simply jibbed at the last moment and the insurance company certainly wouldn't pay out on a mere personal whim.

'I had to explain the rules about cancellation all over again, later, to Mrs Conway,' the assistant added.

Kelsey jerked up in his seat. '*Mrs* Conway?' he repeated.

She nodded. 'Mrs Conway phoned one morning a week or ten days after her husband booked the cruise. I had quite a chat with her. She asked if the cruise had been paid for in full. I told her it had been. She wanted to know what would happen to the money if she cancelled the cruise.'

CHAPTER 24

The assistant cast her mind back. 'I told Mrs Conway it all depended on when the cruise was cancelled. Her husband hadn't taken out any cancellation insurance—I explained why. That meant that any cancellation would come under the contract terms Falcon operate themselves.

'You get all your money back if you cancel at least twenty-eight days before the holiday is due to start. Inside twenty-eight days you start to go into penalty. The penalty increases the nearer you get to the holiday. If you cancel during the last seven days you lose the lot.'

'The whole price of the holiday?'

'That's right.'

'Did Mrs Conway make any comment to all that?'

'No, not really. She just repeated some of what I'd told her, to make sure she'd got it right.'

'How did she sound?'

'Pretty nervy and anxious. I felt sorry for her, she seemed in such a stew over the cruise, terrified of going off on her own. I did my best to jolly her out of it. I told her she'd love it once she got on board, everything would be fine. She'd be very well looked after, everyone would be very kind. She'd soon make friends, there'd be plenty of other folk on their own only too ready to be friendly, there wasn't the slightest need to be nervous. And she still had six weeks or so before the cruise. She'd probably be a lot stronger by then, she'd be feeling more like it, she'd have time to get used to the idea. She had no need to come to any decision in a hurry. It would upset her husband if she did anything impulsive, he'd been so anxious to do what the doctor had suggested, he was so certain the cruise would do her the world of good.'

'How did she take that?'

'It did seem to calm her down. She said: "I'm sure you're right. You must think I'm very silly. I do tend to get things out of proportion since I've not been well." She thanked me for being kind and understanding.'

The assistant raised a hand. 'Oh yes, one other thing—she was most insistent her husband mustn't know she'd phoned. Of course I told her I wouldn't say a word.'

The assistant promised to speak to the manager the moment he returned, get him to phone the Chief right away at Ferndale. If the Chief couldn't be reached there, then the manager should ring the main Cannonbridge police station, ask for the Chief in person.

Before they left, Kelsey asked if he might make a phone call himself. He rang Ferndale and heard the ringing continue for almost two minutes before Conway answered, time enough for Kelsey to begin to sweat again.

'I'd like to come over this morning to clear up a few details,' Kelsey said.

'By all means,' Conway agreed at once. 'What time would suit you?'

The Chief looked at his watch, gave a thought to the distance, the Saturday-morning traffic. 'Eleven-fifteen?' he suggested.

'That'll be fine. I'm off out now but I won't be long. I was getting into the car when I heard the phone ring. I'll be back well before eleven-fifteen.'

In the course of the journey to Oldmoor the Chief uttered not one syllable but leaned back against the upholstery with his eyes closed. Lambert's watch showed eleven-seventeen as they turned in through the bungalow gates. There was no sign of Conway's Zephyr.

Lambert rang the doorbell, rang a second time. And a third. There was no reply. The Chief's face began to assume a stony look.

They went round to the side door, to the back door. They rang and knocked, knocked and rang, without success. Still the Chief hadn't uttered a word.

He began to make a circuit of the house, pressing up against the windows, cupping his hands round his eyes, staring in, searching for signs of upheaval, packing, departure. He could find none. But the whole place had a deserted look. Every door and window secured.

He set off on a tour of the garden. He tried the garage, the doors of sheds. All stood fast against him. He couldn't stay still, he was consumed with the feeling that Conway had outmanœuvred them. He'd done a bunk, he'd had his exit planned all along.

He began another inspection of the house. At the other side of the bathroom window he heard a faint rustling sound, he discerned the pale shape of an imprisoned moth or butterfly beating fruitlessly against the frosted glass.

He went back to where Lambert still stood by the front door. The Chief's brows came together in a massive frown.

'We've left it too late,' he said with bitter certainty. 'I should have known it. Joyce Kimbolt's a far bigger fish than any he's landed so far. He isn't going to miss her if he can help it.'

'He could be stuck in traffic,' Lambert pointed out. 'He could still get here.'

Kelsey gave a savage grunt. 'And pigs may fly.' He retreated into heavy silence, resumed his restless pacing and peering.

Time seemed suspended. A large, dark bird flapped over the garden. A tractor worked in the distance. Cars went by along the main road, never one of them turning into the lane.

All at once Kelsey was halted by a thought. He returned rapidly to Lambert. 'Take the car,' he instructed. He gestured back along the road. 'That phone-box we passed. Ring the estate agent, see if Conway's handed in the keys.'

Lambert was into the car and out through the gates. The minutes crawled by. Yellow leaves drifted down from the trees.

At the sound of a car turning into the lane, Kelsey went to the gate at a rush. But it was only Lambert coming back. He shook his head at the Chief through the windscreen. 'The agent's heard nothing,' he said as he got out of the car. 'The keys haven't been handed in.'

'We'll give him ten more minutes,' the Chief said with grim finality. He had no shred of hope left, he would have been astounded now to see the Zephyr drive in. But he had done with prowling. He felt weary, right down to his bones. He got into the car and leaned back with his eyes closed, waiting for the seconds to tick by. Lambert occupied himself by wandering idly about the garden till the ten minutes were up.

'That's it, then,' the Chief said in leaden tones when Lambert returned to the car. 'Back to Cannonbridge.' He could have wept.

Lambert started up the engine, pulled out into the lane.

The Chief remained sunk in silent gloom, eyes closed, face set in deep lines.

They edged into the main road. A good deal more traffic now.

Lambert suddenly uttered a sharp exclamation. The Chief's eyes shot open.

'There he is!' Lambert gestured out at a car turning out of a junction, coming towards them. Conway's Zephyr. Conway's face visible through the windscreen.

CHAPTER 25

Lambert flashed his lights. Conway looked across and saw them. He raised a hand in greeting. Both cars slid to a halt. Conway got out and came over.

'I don't wonder you'd given me up,' he said in tones of profound apology. 'I'm extremely sorry. I was kept longer than I'd bargained for, then I was twice held up in traffic. Not a damn thing I could do about it.'

The Chief waved his apologies aside. The lines had vanished from his face. His eyes were bright, his voice brisk, he looked ten years younger. 'Forget it. You're here now. We'll follow you back to the house.' A few minutes later Lambert pulled up again by the front door.

'I don't know about you gentlemen, but I'm parched,' Conway said lightly as he let them into the bungalow. 'I could do with a cup of coffee.' There was no sign today in his face or manner of the recent tragedy.

The Chief politely declined the offer. Conway made coffee for himself and carried it into the sitting-room.

'Well, now,' he said in a friendly tone as he settled himself down. 'What is it this time? How can I be of assistance?'

'One or two details that have cropped up,' Kelsey said easily. 'By the way, I'm expecting a phone call. I gave your number, I hope you don't mind.'

'Not at all.' Conway drank his coffee.

'You kept Anna's car in Mrs Egan's garage,' the Chief began. Conway nodded. 'It's my understanding,' the Chief went on, 'that the car was not in the garage at around eight-fifteen on the morning of Monday, October twenty-third.'

Conway began to frown.

'It appears,' the Chief added, 'that the car was away from the garage until some time on Wednesday, October twenty-fifth.'

'I don't know how you arrived at this understanding,' Conway responded with spirit, 'but it's entirely mistaken. Anna's car was very definitely in Mrs Egan's garage at eight-fifteen that Monday morning. It was there all day Monday, Tuesday, Wednesday. It was there all day and every day after that, till I drove it away at the end of my let and sold it.'

'I was given this information by a witness who strikes me as observant and reliable,' the Chief told him imperturbably. 'Not a man given to inventing things.'

'He's got his facts wrong, whoever he is,' Conway retorted with energy. 'The car was never out of the garage for one single instant during those three days. It was never out of the garage at any time during the let for longer than thirty or forty minutes—that was when I took it out for test runs, to see how it was coming along. I suppose I took it out like that four or five times altogether.'

He gave a wry smile. 'The car was properly taxed and insured, all along, if that's what's worrying you. MOT certificate, all in order, check if you like. I didn't break any laws.'

He broke off suddenly, raised a hand. 'I did take the car out for a test run the previous Monday morning, October sixteenth—that could have been when your witness noticed the garage was empty, he just got the week wrong. But the car was back inside the garage half an hour later.'

'What did you do with your own car that Monday

morning while you were out on your test run?' Kelsey asked.
'My witness saw no sign of any other car around.'

'I left it round the back of the garage,' Conway answered
without hesitation. 'Behind some trees, well out of sight, he
wouldn't see it there. I didn't want it stolen or damaged.
Once or twice, early on, I did go to the trouble of locking
it inside the garage while I was out on a run, but I decided
that wasn't really necessary, it was safe enough behind
the trees.'

He gave the Chief a challenging look. 'May I ask who
this witness is?'

The Chief made no response.

'Whoever he is,' Conway pursued, 'he seems to have
nothing better to do than wander about studying the movements of cars and peering into garages. Has he no work to
do? Is he retired, maybe?'

He caught the Chief's expression. He smiled. 'That's it,
isn't it? It's some nosy old pensioner, isn't it? Can you
really credit some old dodderer with such an accurate
memory?' He made a brusquely dismissive gesture. 'He was
telling you what you wanted to hear. Anything to give
himself a bit of importance, put a little excitement into his
life.'

The Chief ignored all that, he came back with another
query. 'Do you intend staying on here at Ferndale?'

Conway shook his head. 'I certainly do not. I'd have got
out at once if I could, it's been a nightmare staying on as
long as this. I'm leaving in a couple of days. I've left my
job as well. I'm getting right away, making a complete
change, putting it all behind me, it's the only thing to do.

'I'm off to Europe, travelling round for a while before I
decide what to do next. If it looks promising over there I
may look round for a suitable opening. I might decide to
stay on for a year or two.'

He gestured abruptly. 'I wasn't going to leave without
telling you. I intended looking in at the station, telling you
my plans, giving you an address where you can get hold of

me. And the name of my bank. I can always be reached through them, I'll be keeping them informed of my whereabouts. I'll be coming back for the inquest, of course, when it's resumed. I'll have to come back anyway, once or twice at least, to settle up Anna's estate.'

'I believe you gave your notice in at Zodiac a week before your wife died,' Kelsey said.

'That's right. I had a disagreement with the sales director. I'd had a couple of clashes with him earlier. He's far too much of a stick-in-the-mud, he ought to be forcibly retired, in my opinion. What they need in that job is a much younger man, someone a lot more go-ahead.' He grimaced. 'He'd got it into his head I was after his job myself.'

He smiled. 'Not that I'd have said no if it had been offered, but there isn't a cat in hell's chance of shifting him before retiring age, he's dug himself in far too well. Anyway, he set out to get rid of me, one way or the other.'

He shrugged. 'Not a lot you can do in that situation when you've only been in a firm five minutes and the other man's determined enough. But I didn't have to stay around to swallow that kind of aggro. Plenty of places in the trade where I can get a job. I gave in my notice on the spur of the moment. I was fed up to the gills that day. He'd been criticizing the way I'd handled a job when there was nothing in the world wrong with it. Of course he was as pleased as Punch when I slapped in my notice, it was what he'd been aiming at.'

'Did you tell your wife you'd given in your notice?'

'I certainly did not. She's the last person I'd have told, she'd have worried herself sick over it. I intended to have a good look round, take my time over it, see how the land really lay inside any other firm I was interested in, before I took the next job. I wasn't going to have a re-run of the Zodiac caper if I could help it. I was sure I'd have fixed myself up with another job, a better job, too, by the time Anna got back from her cruise. Time enough to tell her about it then.'

He fell silent for a moment. 'Then Anna died.' He shook his head. 'The last thing I could think about then was going after other jobs.'

He looked across at Kelsey. 'When I did start to think straight again, I decided to make a complete break, clear out, take some time off, see what I wanted to do with my life.' He shook his head again, slowly. 'Anna's death pulled me up short, it knocked the bottom out of everything. I can't ever see myself going back to the old routine again. It isn't a question of will I or won't I, it just doesn't seem possible any more.'

'Do you think of going into the property business in Europe?' Kelsey asked.

Conway inclined his head. 'I haven't got as far as thinking about particular avenues, but I suppose it's one possibility.'

'Would you be going into business alone? Or with a partner?'

He shrugged. 'There again, too soon to say. I'll be keeping an open mind.'

'Do you think of going into partnership with Miss Kimbolt, perhaps?'

Conway looked baffled. 'Miss Kimbolt?'

'Joyce Kimbolt. You knew her in Northcott, when you worked for Ackroyd's.'

Conway smiled slightly. 'Oh yes, Joyce Kimbolt. Yes, I do remember her. Don't tell me she's in the property business now. I wouldn't have thought her exactly the type.'

'You know her father died? And she inherited everything?'

'No, I didn't know. Well, well, Jack Kimbolt dead. I'd have guessed he had years left in him. He looked as strong as an ox.'

'So you're not contemplating going into the property business in Europe with Joyce Kimbolt?'

Conway laughed. 'I've heard some bright ideas in my time but that beats all.' He laughed again. 'I'll promise you this: if I do happen to run across Joyce Kimbolt in Europe and she suggests it to me, I'll certainly give her my best attention.' He shook his head in lingering amusement. 'Joyce Kimbolt a property developer! I suppose stranger things have happened.'

The Chief switched tack abruptly. 'This cruise Anna was going on—which firm did you book it through?'

Conway's look of amusement vanished but he answered promptly. 'Falcon Travel.'

'A local branch?'

'No, as it happens.' He mentioned the town.

'Why go thirty miles to book the cruise?'

'I didn't go there specially to book the cruise, I was over there on business, I go over there regularly. It wasn't long after Dr Peake suggested a holiday for Anna. I had an hour to spare and I happened to see the branch. I went in to make inquiries, see what was on offer, how much it was likely to cost, pick up a few leaflets. The assistant was very efficient, very helpful, I ended up making the booking then and there, and paying for it.'

'You paid in full?'

'That's right.'

'After Anna died, what steps did you take about the cruise?'

Conway looked haggard again. 'I didn't do anything at first, it went completely out of my head. When I did remember, some days later, I phoned Falcon to say I was cancelling the holiday. That's all I told the girl. I didn't give any reason and I didn't give her time to ask, I was only on the phone a minute or two. I just couldn't face giving any kind of explanation.

'After I'd rung off I thought I'd better put a letter in the post confirming the cancellation. I just said my wife had died suddenly. I realized there was no question of any refund, it was too late for that.

'But a few days later I happened to notice the date on the calendar, November second, the day the cruise began. It crossed my mind that Falcon might have been able to sell the holiday to some last-minute customer. So I wrote to the manager, asking if that was the case, and, if so, would there be any refund.'

He gave the Chief a wry glance. 'That might sound mercenary in the circumstances but I was coming to the end of my job at Zodiac. And it was an expensive cruise—at least I thought it was.'

'Did you get any refund?'

Conway shook his head. 'I haven't heard yet. I expect these things take time.'

'Falcon would surely need to see a death certificate before they'd consider any refund,' Kelsey pointed out.

'Yes, I suppose they would,' Conway responded heavily. 'I hadn't thought of that.' He seemed to sink into himself, he sat gazing down at the carpet.

There was a short silence, then Kelsey asked: 'Does it occur to you at all that Anna may have cancelled the cruise herself?'

Conway's head shot up. His eyes flashed wide, he looked thunderstruck. After some moments he said slowly, in an unsteady voice, 'No, that hadn't occurred to me.'

He stared at Kelsey. 'You're suggesting she could have cancelled it the day—' He broke off, then steadied himself and went on. 'The day she died?'

'It's possible,' Kelsey said. 'Or she could have cancelled it earlier.'

Conway put a hand up to his face. 'What you're suggesting,' he said after another pause, 'is that she couldn't face telling me she'd cancelled it.'

He looked at the Chief with anguished eyes. 'She was standing there. Garbutt was asking about the cruise. I told him I was taking her shopping for her clothes, driving her down to Southampton.' He drew a trembling breath. 'She must have felt it all closing in on her. She could see only one way out.'

'It's no more than a supposition,' the Chief pointed out. 'It may have no basis whatever in fact.'

Conway said nothing but gazed down at the floor with a stricken face.

There was another laden silence, broken suddenly by the phone ringing in the front hall.

The Chief rose swiftly to his feet. 'I expect that's for me,' he told Conway.

Conway appeared scarcely to hear. After a moment he glanced up and gave a nod. The Chief went from the room, shutting the door behind him.

Conway made no attempt to speak to Sergeant Lambert while the Chief was gone. He slumped down in his chair and closed his eyes. It was some time before the Chief came back. He thought at first that Conway had fallen asleep but he stirred and opened his eyes as the Chief took his seat again.

'Is this likely to take much longer?' Conway asked. He sounded like a man drawing on his last reserves of energy.

'Not much longer,' the Chief assured him. 'One or two things still to get straight.'

Conway drew a deep breath and gave a resigned nod. He levered himself into a more upright position.

'You expected your wife to begin her cruise on November second?' Kelsey began briskly.

Conway uttered a groan. 'Must we go into all this again? You must know it off by heart by now.'

'If you would just answer yes or no,' the Chief responded equably. 'Then we can get on all the faster.'

'Yes,' Conway said between his teeth. 'I did expect Anna to begin her cruise on November second.'

'You intended to drive her to Southampton?'

Conway kept a tight grip on his patience. 'Yes. And I was going to meet her there on her return.'

'You had arranged to take her into Cannonbridge on the Wednesday afternoon, October twenty-fifth, to buy her clothes for the cruise?'

'That's right.'

'Some days after her death you rang Falcon to cancel the booking?'

'I did.'

'Later that same day you posted a letter to the branch manager, confirming the cancellation, telling him your wife had died suddenly?'

'That is so.' The muscles stiffened along Conway's jaw.

'And some days after that, on November second, you again wrote to the manager, asking if Falcon had been able to sell the holiday, if there was any possibility of a refund?'

'Yes, I did.'

Kelsey contemplated him for some moments. 'This is where I find myself at something of a loss.' He took his notebook from his pocket. 'That was the Falcon manager on the phone just now, the manager of the branch where you booked the cruise.'

Conway sat very still. His eyes grew bright and hard.

'I made notes of our conversation,' the Chief continued in the same even tone. 'To avoid any possibility of mistake or misunderstanding.'

He glanced up at Conway, down again at his notebook. 'This is what the manager tells me. First, that he received no letter from you at any time after your wife's death. Nor can he find any record of any phone call made by you after your wife's death, cancelling the cruise.'

Conway sat like an image hewn from granite.

Kelsey glanced briefly up again and then went on. 'The manager further says that he would have been very surprised indeed to receive such a phone call or letters from you, in view of the fact that you had called in personally at the branch and cancelled the cruise, on Friday, September twenty-ninth. More than three weeks before your wife's death.'

CHAPTER 26

Conway stared fixedly at the opposite wall.

'You spoke to the counter clerk when you called in,' Kelsey said. 'The clerk referred you to the manager. You explained to the manager in some detail that your wife had changed her mind about the cruise. Some friends had very kindly offered to take her with them for a month to their villa in Portugal where she would be able to convalesce in peace and quiet. She jumped at the offer, she was delighted not to have to go off on holiday on her own.

'In the circumstances you regretted you must cancel the cruise. As you were giving more than a month's notice of cancellation you asked for the full return of your money in accordance with Falcon's contract terms.'

Conway made no sound, no stir.

'The manager further tells me,' Kelsey continued, 'that he spent some time trying to persuade you not to take the refund but to use the money to book another holiday for later on, a holiday for you and your wife together, perhaps. But he had no success, you insisted on the refund. So he wrote you out a cheque for the full amount and handed it over to you there and then.'

He fixed Conway with a steely eye. 'The manager is ready to go into court to swear to all this. He can produce all the relevant paperwork. Including the receipt you signed and dated, for the full refund.'

Conway's eyes never left the wall.

'You were happy to play the generous husband,' Kelsey went on. 'Booking an expensive holiday for your ailing wife, offering to buy her new clothes—knowing all along you'd never be out of pocket from any of it by so much as one single penny.

'Anna finally reached a point where she had got used to

the idea of going off on holiday on her own. She was no longer afraid of it, she was looking forward to it, believed she would enjoy it, was pleased at the thought of choosing new outfits. You played along with all that, right to the end. You knew Anna would never be going shopping for new clothes, you'd never be driving her to Southampton. You cancelled the holiday weeks before it was due to start because you knew full well Anna would never be going on the cruise. You were certain of that because you planned to kill her on the morning of Monday, October twenty-third. And on that Monday morning, kill her you did, in cold blood.

'That night, while Anna lay in the mortuary, you sat at the table in the interview room, working out what you'd do with the money her death had brought you.'

Silence descended on the room. Conway sat rigid.

Kelsey leaned forward. 'You never forgot the lesson you learned as a lad, working at the manor. I've not the slightest doubt Biddulph's niece and her boyfriend took the old man up on to the scaffolding and pushed him off, though there isn't a snowball's chance in hell of proving it now. Murder for profit—you realized how it had been done, how easily everyone had swallowed it. It made a deep impression on you, you saw it could be a very enticing game. Only needed a little care and planning, a little patience in setting up the right scenario, waiting for the right moment. You saw it was a game you could very easily take to yourself. All you needed was the right opportunity.'

Conway betrayed not the slightest flicker of response.

'You went to work at Bredon House,' Kelsey pursued. 'You met Ida Willett, you realized you'd found your opportunity. You laid your plans, you murdered Ida. You got away with it. It put some money in your pocket. Not a fortune, but a start. Next time it might be more.

'You came across Anna, you saw the possibilities with Reardon, the chance of pocketing a larger sum. You never loved Anna for one single instant, you merely made use of

her to get at Reardon's money. You conned her into marrying Reardon. It was your idea all the way, never hers.'

He jabbed at the air. 'It was never Anna who refused to
buy a house on mortgage, never Anna who insisted on
having the money for a cash purchase. That was always
your ploy, to persuade her into marrying Reardon. Anna
would cheerfully have married you and gone to live with
you in your bachelor flat, she'd have lived with you in a
tent if that was what you wanted.

'You persuaded her that marrying Reardon would work
out for the best all round. It wouldn't be a full, normal
marriage, and you would still go on seeing her while she
was married to Reardon. He needn't know about it and
what he didn't know wouldn't hurt him. She could ease any
qualms she felt by giving Reardon the best of care. He
couldn't live more than a year or two, then she could marry
you, use her inheritance to buy a house for the pair of you,
that would be her contribution to your life together. She
could always be proud of that, knowing she'd earned her
inheritance by giving Reardon the comfort and happiness
he needed in the final part of his life.

'She agreed to the marriage with Reardon in all good
faith. She swallowed your ploy, hook, line and sinker. She
never for one instant guessed what you really had in mind
for him. She'd have agreed to anything you suggested, she
loved you devotedly, she was terrified of losing you. She was
a simple, unsophisticated girl, she hadn't the faintest notion
of the twists and turns of a mind like yours.'

The Chief struck his fist into his palm. 'You murdered
Reardon entirely by yourself, without any assistance,
any connivance, any knowledge whatsoever on the part of
Anna.'

Conway gave a sudden snort of laughter. 'Much use any
assistance from Anna would have been,' he said with savage
derision. 'She'd have fainted with fright at the thought of
such a thing.'

'It was always part of your plan to murder Anna when

the time came.' Kelsey's voice was harsh and icy. 'You heard Jack Kimbolt had died, you knew the time to murder Anna had come. You set about planning her death in earnest. You had no intention of losing Joyce Kimbolt's money if you could help it.'

Conway regarded him with a sardonic half-smile.

'There's no chance now of getting you for Ida Willett's death,' Kelsey said with fierce regret. 'Not after this length of time. Or for Reardon's death. We won't even be trying.' His eyes burned into Conway. 'But as sure as hell we'll get you for the murder of Anna. You're a mighty glib talker and you're a first-class liar. Some of your lies may take a bit of unravelling. But there's no way on this earth you're going to be able to talk your way out of Anna's murder.'

Conway's smile vanished. He turned a ferocious glare on Kelsey. 'She was a stupid, romantic fool!' He spat out the words with vitriolic contempt. 'That's what they all were—gullible, romantic fools. They'd swallow any half-likely tale you cared to feed them. All they wanted was love. Love!' He gave another snort of laughter. 'Sitting ducks, the lot of them. What use was a single one of them to a living soul? Is there a creature on the face of the earth the worse off that any of them's dead?'

From the mantelpiece Anna looked out at him with her radiant smile.

'I've not the faintest doubt,' Kelsey flung at him, 'that Joyce Kimbolt would have gone the way of Ida and Anna. You'd have murdered her when you'd done with her, as you murdered the others. She'll have plenty to say when she discovers the truth of your little game. And she'll say it loud and clear, make no mistake about that.'

Conway threw back at him a look of insolent challenge. 'You may have put paid to my little game but that won't save your precious Miss Kimbolt. You can't put a guard round her for the rest of her life. Some punter will have her one fine day, you can lay good money to that. There's no law ever made can protect females like Joyce Kimbolt. Natural born fools.'

A little later, as they were all three standing in the front hall about to leave for the police station, the Chief suddenly remembered the imprisoned butterfly.

He went along to the bathroom. The butterfly was perched on the window-sill, able now to manage no more than an occasional feeble flutter. Its frail white wings were delicately veined with green.

Kelsey opened the transom, cupped the trembling creature with infinite gentleness in his great hands. He felt life throb against his skin. He bore it up to the current of air, spread his fingers wide.

It quivered against his palm. Its wings began to vibrate, they beat more steadily, more strongly. It rose a little, hovered, rose again. Then it was out and away, soaring through the pale gold sunshine into its fleeting day.

He closed the transom and stood for a moment glancing about the room. There was no shower fitment. He gazed down at the bath. Every single day since that Monday morning Conway would have stepped into that bath.

As he went back along the passage he noticed the sitting-room door standing ajar. He paused by the threshold.

On the mantelpiece a ray of sunlight gilded Anna's photograph. He crossed to the hearth and looked down at that childlike face, its expression immutably fixed in the happiness of that seaside day. Behind his eyes he felt the terrible press of unshed tears. He put out a finger and touched the glassy cheek.

'We nailed him for you, Anna,' he said softly. 'We nailed him for you in the end.'

He turned and went from the room, closing the door on those artless eyes, that unfading smile.

In the silent hall the other two stood waiting, Conway with a face carved from stone, his hands at his sides, fists tight clenched.

They went out into the bright November day, rooks calling, a flurry of rusty leaves whirling in the breeze. Above their heads the pale blue expanse of sky was streaked with snowy, spreading vapour trails, marking the passage of some jet plane long since vanished from view.